MW01126231

PIECE OF DRAGON

HARET CHRONICLES QILIN: BOOK ONE

LAUREL CHASE

Copyright © 2018 Laurel Chase

All rights reserved.

LaurelChaseAuthor.com

This is a work of fiction. Names, characters, businesses, places, events and incidents are either the products of the author's imagination or used in a fictitious manner. Any resemblance to actual persons, living or dead, or actual events is purely coincidental.

Cover design by

Christian Bentulan

ISBN: 9781723829277

DEDICATION

This book is for all the girls who like sex and sugar.

So, that's everyone, right?

Carry on.

CHAPTER ONE

CARLYLE

I stood motionless in the shade of a maple tree, scanning the festival crowd as it surged into activity. My long, white-blond hair was heavy on my neck in the July humidity, and the scent of fried foods and spun sugar floated thickly in the mid-summer air. The two-lane Main Street was packed with booths and folding tables loaded with baked goods and canned drinks, handmade holiday decorations, and crafts of all kinds.

I focused on the festival's early innocence, drinking in the people's illusion of carefree fun and freedom, the laugh and "howdy" of neighbors greeting each other.

Before the night was over, those smells would turn to sweat and desperation, and I'd be sleeping off a powerful depression after a night of work.

Festival life wasn't easy, but it was the life I'd carved for myself after running away from foster care five years before. I was a hell of a lot better off now than I'd ever been - no bills or commitments tying me down, my business partner LuAnn for easy company, and enough money for gas, food, and coffee. I could even get cotton candy whenever I wanted.

The biggest reason I kept moving, though, was that I needed to stay one step ahead of the Ringmaster and his recruiters. He ran the infamous Underbelly Circus, and he wanted me enough that I'd already dodged his people twice.

My attention was drawn to a pack of guys bouncing past my tree. They were shouting and laughing about their coming drunken night, and I shrunk further into the shadows.

I was only here to observe the crowd - to see, not to be seen.

Only one glanced my way, and I startled as his golden eyes flashed and locked on mine instantly. Damn, he was a beautiful one - all power and grace, whispers and dynamite. A small hum of appreciation escaped my lips, and I clamped my mouth shut around it.

He couldn't possibly have heard me, but he held my gaze captive for several steps. I almost ducked and slid behind the rough trunk to break the connection. A stare like that was one humanity lived or died by - an instinctual challenge to either fight or fuck.

It had been a long time since I'd had to do one or allowed myself to do the other.

The group passed on quickly, their bravado and

excitement stinking up the air with a musk like fresh blood. To me, people's emotions had scents as different as fingerprints. Interpreting and manipulating them at LuAnn's festival booth put cash in my pocket, but these personal scents were also a fascination - a whole different dimension of the people-watching I loved so much.

The flame-haired guy turned his golden eyes forward again, and I was relieved as I took one final glance at his broad shoulders and cocky swagger. I didn't need that temptation tonight. I had work to do.

A younger-looking boy broke from the group, flipping both middle fingers back at the others when they jeered. He stalked my way without even looking, aggravation pulling his brows together. None of his friends followed - perfect.

I left the shelter of the tree and fell in step just behind him, matching my soft steps to the clump of his shiny cowboy boots. Reaching the railing overlooking the river, he smacked his hands on the handrail. Careful to keep several feet away, I leaned on the railing next to the boy and inhaled the rusted metal swirls of his anger and frustration.

I fluffed my pale, wavy hair so it tumbled around my shoulders and all the way down my back. The boy was still glaring daggers at the horizon. He wasn't as young as I'd thought, but he would still do.

"Hey," I said, using the soft, flirty voice that always seemed to work on the angry ones.

He turned and blinked at me twice, taking in my lavender-blue eyes and easy smile. His scowl receded as he focused on me. "Hey." His eyes wandered my curves, but I ignored it.

3

"Nice day for a festival," I said, turning my gaze back to the river, which was slow-moving and swollen with rain.

"Do you live around here?" he asked, slanting closer. "Never seen you before."

"Nope." I grinned at his small-town logic, keeping my eyes on the lapping water. He'd never see my ass again, either. "Just in for the festival." I pulled a stack of palm-sized advertisements from the pocket of my cut-offs and flapped them at my neck to create a pointless breeze.

"Are you selling something?" he asked, reaching for a paper.

"Aren't we all?" I replied with a smirk. He chuckled - the boys I approached always liked that statement.

I slid an ad to him, careful not to touch my bare fingers with his. I didn't want any of his emotions to accidentally rub off on me.

As he read the paper, his smile grew into a teasing grin. "You're a hypnotist?" he asked, laughter creeping into his voice.

I lifted a shoulder, keeping a blank face and repressing my annoyance. "I just work for one. But she doesn't make you do stupid tricks. Lady Ezmeralda uses hypnosis to find your hidden emotions. Then she tells them to go the fuck away so you can enjoy your life again."

Of course, Lady Ezmeralda was really just LuAnn in a cheap costume, but she was pretty good at putting people under so I could do my work in secret. That way, nobody asked questions about my unique abilities.

The boy gave a surprised sort of laugh as he tried to hand the paper back to me.

I flicked my fingers at him. "Keep it. I have hundreds more to pass out today." I pulled my thick hair over one shoulder, trying to get a bit more air on my neck. The humidity was brutal.

"So you just do the advertising?" he asked, clicking together what he thought were the answers. Good boy, following the breadcrumbs I'd dropped.

"Something like that. Usually I find someone to split the job with. Makes it go faster, so I can have some fun." Lie, lie, lie, and he ate it right up. I never had any fun the first night of a festival - only the last.

"You paying?" he asked, and I grinned. Finally. He'd followed the trail to its perfect end. Then again, it was my job to make sure they did.

"Fifty bucks," I offered, keeping my voice low like it was a secret.

"Fifty? To hand out a bunch of paper?" He sounded doubtful. Small-town logic again.

I only nodded, shoving the ads into my back pocket again. I noticed a flash of movement over his shoulder. The flame-haired guy stood at the edge of the crowd, watching me. His sharp gaze made me nervous. The Ringmaster had never sent a guy after me before, but it was totally possible this guy was a recruiter.

Underbelly recruiting was really more like kidnapping, though.

I turned back to the boy before me. I needed to leave if he wasn't in.

"We make enough," I said, pushing off the railing. "So, you want in or not?" I asked, growing impatient as he looked me over again. Despite my curvy figure, I had a baby face and was only a few inches above five feet. I could intimidate when I wanted to, though, and I shot him a bitchy look.

He cocked his head, still skeptical, then shrugged. "Sure, what the hell."

"We start now," I added, and he nodded. I passed the ads to him and began firing instructions. "I'll pay you when we're done. You hand these out. I'll follow. Don't make eye contact with me - they don't need to know we're a team. Go slow so I can keep up. Only one per couple or group. No little kids. And watch especially for the ones having too much fun, or not enough."

"Too much fun?" he scoffed, shuffling the papers into a neater stack.

"It leads to desperation," I said, glancing back at the river. "It's the same everywhere," I added under my breath. I walked toward the crowd, scanning the people for that bright red hair.

"What do I say to them? To get them to go see you?" he called, his boots clicking on the sidewalk as he hurried to catch up.

I shrugged. "It doesn't matter. That's my part."

To his credit, he followed my instructions to the letter. I slunk behind him, keeping my distance to watch how people reacted when they received the advertisement. Certain reactions always stood out - the people most likely to agree to one of the "adjustments" LuAnn and I sold.

That's where my night really began. As I passed each one, I brushed their bare arms with whisper-soft fingers. Using my odd power, I pushed and pulled at their emotions, heightening and twisting the ugliest ones.

Some of them, I jostled and cursed at fluently when they jostled me back. *Anger.*

Some, I looked up and down appreciatively, fluffing my long, white-gold hair and watching them with sly glances as I sauntered away. *Desire.*

Others, I siphoned away the false joy the festival was bringing to their tedious lives, leaving only the sense that this day really was just like all the others. *Desperation.*

A select few I simply pick-pocketed.

I only stole from the assholes - they would never come to our tent anyway. By the time we doubled back to the river, the boy was empty-handed, and I had more than enough cash to pay him.

"Thanks for your help," I said, sliding him some of the stolen money. I was already tired from manipulating people's emotions, and I was jittery from watching out for the flame-haired guy. I'd glimpsed him a couple of times as I'd worked the crowd, but each time I'd managed to lose myself in a group.

The boy grinned and stepped closer like we weren't done. I held my ground, hoping he wouldn't touch me. "So, I need to be checking in with my boss now. Come by the tent later if you want," I offered as I turned away.

"Hey, what's your name?" he called after me. His disappointment was evident in the earthy scent of rot.

"Carlyle," I answered, just before ducking into a large group of people.

I wove through the crowd until I found a less-crowded spot in the street. I relaxed with my back to a brick wall for a few minutes. Scanning the crowd one final time, I decided the redhead must have moved on.

I breathed in deeply to clear the emotions from my nose, noticing that much of the festival's early afternoon sweetness had already been replaced by grilled meat and onions, overtaxed bathrooms, and plastic cups of warm beer. The sun had sunk close to the river, and I still needed to shore up my happiness before night swept through the crowd and the most difficult part of my job began.

True happiness was a difficult emotion to find, though.

Vendors' pleasure at sales could quickly grow into greed. A young couple's first date often disintegrated into jealousy over someone else's bare summer skin. But I hadn't lied to the boy about my skill. Even though I'd never met another person with an ability like mine, I was damn good at what I did.

So, when I spotted a grandma-type on a park bench, smiling at a child playing in the grass, I settled next to her to begin stealing bits of the woman's happiness for myself. For me, it was as simple and quick as pickpocketing.

Even though I couldn't steal happiness from the assholes, I was always careful not to take too much from anyone. I knew how dangerous my power could be, and I never wanted to hurt anyone else with the weird skill I had.

CHAPTER TWO

JACK

"So… Jack, is it, this time?" the Ringmaster asked, digging his thick fingers into my temples as I held myself still and silent. My arms were tense and pale as I fisted my hands at my sides.

He didn't need to touch people to read their thoughts. The asshole just enjoyed how concrete pain enhanced the nausea that came with him digging through my memories.

"Interesting choice of names for this cycle. Jack be nimble, Jack be quick. Something about a candlestick, I think. Will you get burned, Jack, when you jump? You do love to jump."

I clenched my teeth against the growing ache in my skull, but I didn't flinch. I never flinched, and this was why the Ringmaster hated me the most. He respected me for it, too, though respect got you nowhere in the Underbelly Circus.

The Ringmaster removed his grip from my face and slowly pulled back his invisible mental probes. Slouching back in the ridiculous medieval throne we carried from city to city, the Ringmaster eyed me, pinning my blue eyes with his black ones. He ran his palms down the slick silk of his tie, straightening it. "I have another job for you. This one is different. I *need* her."

The psychotic fervor in the man's eyes wasn't helping a damn bit with my nausea.

"What's in it for me?" I said after managing to catch enough breath to speak evenly. My last big job had earned me a new mattress. I scrubbed at my coarse brown hair, standing it up even more than usual in my efforts to rub away his touch. "Unless you're ready to set me free," I cracked, not bothering to hide the bitter edge of my tone.

I'd been in the Circus long enough to forget where I was before. I'd picked a new name so many times I couldn't even remember my first one. None of my new identities had made a difference, though. The Ringmaster's tricks and powers were legendary: I'd never escape the Underbelly Circus, and neither would any of the recruits I'd ever been sent to retrieve.

With my unique powers, I couldn't even escape the Ringmaster in death. I'd simply start another cycle, right where the last one had ended.

Immortality wasn't that cool if it was indentured.

The Ringmaster leaned forward and smiled at me, cruel and slow. "If you find her and bring her back unharmed, you can have the thing you'll want most."

"And what is that?" I asked, lifting an eyebrow at his use of future tense. I scratched at my two-day stubble, wishing we were done with this meeting already. Out of habit, I twisted the gold ring on my thumb, its weight and purity giving me a certain comfort that a mattress never could. "I'm resigned to this life."

I totally fucking wasn't, but it was all part of the act.

"Not your fate." The Ringmaster grinned wider, showing his double row of perfect white teeth. "The girl's."

"*Her* life is what I most want?" I said, dangerously close to scoffing. The Ringmaster waited, the edge of a nod in the incline of his sharp jaw. His top hat was low over his dark eyes now, shadowing his olive skin. I sighed without making a sound. "I'd still rather have mine."

"Your life is worth nothing."

I scowled. How true it was. But avoiding pain was worth something, which the Ringmaster knew too well. I'd resisted before, but I wasn't about to ask for another round of torture for no good reason.

"Why is this girl so important?" I asked, stalling for time to lock those memories down tight. My fingers fidgeted with the ragged hem of my t-shirt, and I forced them to still.

"If you jump, will your little candle burn you? Hurt you when it counts the most?" the Ringmaster said, reverting back to his riddles and games instead of answering the question.

Then his power flashed forward, his mind squeezing mine so tightly that I could do nothing, think nothing, not even blink or breathe or struggle. My world was nothing but pain and his words echoing in every pulse. "If you find her, Jack, she will be your greatest strength. Your biggest fear. Your worst weakness. Your light in the dark, dark world. Even though you think you have all the fire in your own belly, hers burns *hotter*."

The Ringmaster released his hold abruptly and casually offered me a slip of paper, a bored look on his ageless face. Heaving and clenching my muscles to stop the shaking, I took the damn paper.

There was no more point in discussing it; we both knew I would do the job. I shoved it in my jeans pocket without looking, knowing it would have the last-known coordinates of some poor kid I was now charged with recruiting.

That wasn't the right word, though.

It was always more like kidnapping.

I swiveled and left the sleek luxury RV that served as the Ringmaster's traveling home, blinking as I stepped into the bright afternoon sun.

All around me seethed the stuff of rebellion. Circus folk - my folk - sought the freedom of the road, living off the grid, testing their strength and bravery nightly for a new group of wide-eyed, peanut-munching families.

Yet I always wondered how nobody noticed what Underbelly itself lacked. Circuses over the centuries had been family-based, but there was nothing of that here. This circus was too full of young, beautiful people with fragile smiles. Older adults were scarce. The animals' behavior, if you watched closely enough, was just a little too human. The acts themselves… well, some were just a little too impossible.

Everyone believed because they wanted to believe.

Underbelly was famous for all the right reasons, and

home to its performers for all the wrong reasons.

My long legs eating up the distance, I strode past the wavy line of compact utility tents and storage trucks, deep into the grid of animal cages. Certain members of the Underbelly Circus were simply too dangerous and disloyal to walk the grounds.

"Handsome Jack," a voice hissed through the nearest bars. "I'm lonely. Come play a bit."

I rolled my eyes. Arcadia was beautiful, but all she did was play vicious games. I'd grown tired of trying to help her months ago. "Not today, *harpy*."

The word got the reaction it always did. The special steel bars sparked as the black-haired girl inside smacked her arms against them. The air crackled with electricity and seemed to shimmer around her, a faint shadow of unformed wings on the back of the cage. Her dark eyes narrowed at me in disgust, even as she offered me a twisted grin.

I kept walking, careful to keep more than an arm's length from her cage. She wouldn't be a problem much longer. Her earn-back period should be up in less than a year.

Then the Ringmaster would allow her the ultimate gamble: Life or Liberty. The remaining years of her life, for the magic in her soul, or the freedom to walk away, if she could.

They always picked Life.

This meant the Ringmaster always won the game, but only I knew just what he was winning. I was the only one in the Circus who had seen the Portal the Ringmaster was building.

Well, maybe not the only one. I paused, scanning the

rows of decrepit cages for the one I needed. Other hooded eyes tracked my movements from the dark depths of their cages, and other bars rattled with menace. As the Ringmaster's main recruiter, I'd earned very few friends.

Finally, I saw the kid I wanted, hunched in the corner of a medium-sized enclosure, tucked away from the slanting sun. A book of poetry lay closed in his lap: *Paradise Lost*.

"Not today, *dragon*," the young boy said, mocking my words of just a few minutes before. "Your future won't be decided today."

"What does that mean, Austin?" I asked, keeping my voice low. I pulled a handful of wrapped candies from my pocket and tossed them through the bars. Austin wasn't dangerous. He wasn't caged because of violence or vitriol.

He was caged because he was the only one the Ringmaster couldn't control with his mental probes.

"Just because the Ringmaster is offering you a choice, doesn't mean you have to pick one of his choices. There are always options we don't see. Even me," the boy added, shoving a candy in his mouth and pushing the wrapper through a crack in the plank floor. It fell silently to the grass beneath the cage.

"What's her name?" Austin asked.

"Can't you see it?" I teased, tugging the paper from my jeans pocket.

Austin didn't answer, only added a second candy to his mouth, puffing out both pale cheeks.

"Carlyle," I read, tracing a finger over the name. The coordinates weren't familiar, but I knew the general location. Smack in the middle of nowhere. I sighed. Small town hell.

"She's pretty, I think," Austin mumbled, his light eyes half-closed. "And really, like, new."

"New?"

Austin shrugged. "Like she doesn't know much, I think." He was still learning his powers. Sometimes his clairvoyance was clear, and sometimes it was like looking through a foggy glass.

"Anything else?" I asked, impatience flickering across my chest. I always asked Austin for advice before recruiting, and usually the kid was more help than this.

Austin swallowed the candy and grinned, leaning back to scratch his bald head against the wood of the cage. "She's dangerous. When she finds out the truth, she'll burn us all down."

A thrill raced up my spine as I realized how closely-matched Austin's prediction was to the Ringmaster's. A girl who was beautiful and dangerous? Underbelly had that in spades.

But a girl who was a threat to someone like me? Or to the Ringmaster himself?

That would be worth jumping for.

"Now go play with Arcadia," Austin muttered, his grin slipping. "Today's her day."

I snapped my attention back to the kid. "Today? She has months left."

Austin shrugged, just as a vicious cackle of laughter echoed off the cages. I bolted for Arcadia's cage.

CHAPTER THREE

JACK

Arcadia was smacking the bars and stomping her bare feet on the metal floor of her cage. Slivers of something like lightning lit the inside of the cage. She shrieked an insult when she saw me round the corner, then turned and unleashed a string of ugly curses at the tall man standing before the cage.

The Ringmaster watched her calmly, swinging his black cane in gentle arcs across the grass, beheading the weeds as it went. Despite the summer heat and his full tuxedo, he wasn't sweating a bit.

I pulled up short. I was too late now to do anything but watch the show.

In the nearby cages, kids and creatures pushed their

faces to the bars, anxious to watch one of their own battle for her life. Even several who were free to roam the grounds had gathered, peeking around the corners of cages, but ready to sprint back to safety if things went wrong.

Some of the newer recruits had never witnessed this ritual, and even my cynical, scabbed heart ached for what I knew they were all about to see. I pushed a few of the littler ones behind my tall form, hoping to block their view. Edging closer to Arcadia's cage, I raked my hand through my messy dark hair in frustration.

I didn't like her, and I doubted my presence would be a comfort, but I didn't want this for her, either.

The Ringmaster stopped swinging his cane and pushed the tip into the soft earth. "You'll never earn back what I've spent on you, Arcadia. Those special bars are expensive, you know."

"I still have eleven months," she hissed. The shadow of wings was growing darker, spooling from her back like smoke. It was impressive, really, that she was so close to transforming even inside the spelled cage.

"No, Arcadia. I have the record here. You agreed to a reduced earning period to save your sister. Your signature," the Ringmaster pointed to a scrawl on the page of a slim, leather-bound book. Arcadia howled in rage and slammed against the cage so fiercely that a bar cracked.

Sneering with hate, she did it again. And again. And again, until her palms were bloodied and the bars were bent just enough for her to squeeze through.

She locked her dark eyes with my blue ones, her emotions impossible to read, just before she shot out of the cage and up, up into the cloudless sky. Several of the watching performers gasped at her power, and seeing her transform tickled something in my memory.

She could have been a hawk or an eagle. As she wheeled above us, someone might have even mistaken her for a vulture. She could have escaped. But the Ringmaster sighed, and my heart sank as she began to plummet back toward us, intent on knocking the life from the man who had stolen hers.

"Harpies never learn," the Ringmaster murmured, disappointment flashing in his eyes. I knew the moment he locked onto her mind, because her form stiffened and spread wide. She resembled a traitor on a king's rack, being pulled into four quarters. Only her wings beat, the motion painfully slow, like smoke curling and drifting in a still sky.

The circus was silent. Everyone was either watching or trying not to watch.

And even though I'd never liked Arcadia much, I hated the Ringmaster with a passion so intense I could barely breathe.

"Oh, Jack," the man whispered, sensing my thoughts. "One day, you'll see. One day, I pray you'll recognize me for the savior I am."

"You are a murderer," I bit out, unable to tear my eyes from Arcadia's frozen form, floating in mid-air fifty feet above us.

The Ringmaster blinked, taking his eyes from the sky to study me, and Arcadia fell like a stone. Fuck, I hadn't meant for that to happen. She didn't make a sound as she crashed to the ground, and neither did anyone watching. The silence only highlighted the snap of bones breaking and the squishing rupture of internal organs.

I thought I heard a whimper behind me, but I didn't

dare turn and draw attention to the mistake. The rules of Underbelly were absolute, and pity was not welcome in this act.

The Ringmaster knelt on one knee beside the broken harpy, the tails of his immaculate black silk coat brushing the stiff summer grass. "Life or Liberty?" he asked, just as always.

Arcadia's eyes flickered, and I knew she was on the brink of choosing neither. Choosing oblivion. However, just as the Ringmaster controlled our lives, so did he control our deaths.

"A scale, Jack," he said crisply, holding a hand out behind him as the girl's wings shimmered and shrunk to nothing. She was slight, barely seventeen, and shattered.

I'd known this was coming, and I hated every shred of myself for doing as I was asked. She didn't deserve this. Choking down my self-disgust, I reached under my shirt and shifted out a claw, scratching harshly at the skin along my spine. The pain was there as always, but I didn't register it. Blood trickled down my skin, but I didn't staunch it.

My stomach fluttered as I pulled at a bit of myself. There was a wet, popping noise, and finally a slimed scale, no bigger than a fingernail, broke off into my palm.

I shuddered and slapped it, gore and all, into the Ringmaster's outstretched hand.

"Thank you, my good servant," the Ringmaster said. The humor in his voice nearly made me scream. I forced myself to stay silent, waiting for Arcadia's answer. I knew what she would choose, but I always hoped one day... one day someone would choose something else.

The Ringmaster pushed her body flat without

19

ceremony and produced a scalpel from his inner jacket pocket.

"Life or Liberty?" he asked Arcadia again.

She heaved, coughing up a stream of blood that trickled down her cheek. One of her legs was bent backward beneath her, and blood soaked through her jeans.

"Life," she rasped, her face distorted in pain.

The Ringmaster smiled. It was a smile born from decades of triumph, and I didn't have to be a mind reader to feel the fear and loathing seeping from the watching people. I twisted the gold ring on my thumb again, needing its comfort for what was coming next.

The Ringmaster bent down further and sliced open the front of Arcadia's bloodied t-shirt, pushing the fabric away from her ribcage. He made a precise incision in her chest, just beneath the left ribs.

A cut he'd practiced dozens and dozens of times.

Arcadia shuddered but didn't cry out, and I appreciated her bravery. Although, if she'd truly been brave, she would have chosen Liberty and been done with this place forever.

The Ringmaster slipped a finger inside her chest cavity, drawing out what looked like a rounded box carved of bone. He used the scalpel to slice away the bloody tendons holding the box to her insides, then he slipped my scale into the empty space. He wiped his fingers and the scalpel on a black cloth from his pocket.

Arcadia breathed a shaky sigh of relief as the scale began to root. I knew the pain would recede quickly. My dragon scale would heal her body, bringing back the life she'd bargained for in desperation.

It didn't matter. The Ringmaster had what he wanted

now: Harpy magic was a cornerstone of the Portal he was building, bit by magical bit.

Smashing the fragile bone box in his fist, the Ringmaster stood, clutching something none of us could see.

"A nice blue. Like the summer sky," Austin called, his voice startling in the silence.

The Ringmaster turned toward the kid's cage and smiled. "Your powers are growing stronger. Excellent."

Rustling and whispers began. Underbelly knew generally what our master collected, but not why. He opened his fingers and held his hand up. In his palm rested a small blue shard, something like beach glass. But this shard pulsed with magic.

Only I knew it was another piece to the puzzle that was the Ringmaster's Portal.

The Ringmaster had told me once the Portal was open, the entire world would change. I wasn't certain that would be a bad thing, and it was one reason I continued to collect for the man I hated.

It was true that the Ringmaster was evil, but a world that didn't notice the evil right before their eyes was surely worse.

Arcadia stumbled to her feet, clutching her shirt closed. Everyone stepped out of her way as she limped away slowly, stiffly, in the direction of the administration tent. Now, she'd be assigned a trailer like mine and a new place in the Underbelly Circus, or perhaps granted a transfer to one of the Ringmaster's other compounds around the world.

She had her life, and she would heal, but now the Ringmaster had her magic. She'd never fly again.

I watched her, feeling the strange corkscrew pull I always did after giving away another scale. The Ringmaster had promised me I'd never run out, but I wondered. What exactly was I giving them? What was I losing each time I put a piece of my regeneration power to use inside someone else?

"Don't you have somewhere to be?" the Ringmaster barked, turning to me. He motioned to my pocket containing the girl's coordinates. "And you others?" he addressed the gathered crowd. "Busy yourselves. We have a show to put on tonight."

"And the show must go on," Austin called mockingly, eliciting nervous, relieved laughter from the young performers.

CHAPTER FOUR

CARLYLE

When LuAnn opened our booth for the night, I was ready - energized by the good vibes I'd stolen from unsuspecting strangers and munching on my first bag of cotton candy.

LuAnn sat in the tent's shadows, white pillar candles lighting her olive skin and shiny curls with a beauty most small towns only saw in the movies. She wore a swirling dress of bright colors, a scarf in her hair, and tinkling jewelry, perpetuating the stereotype that sold so, so well.

I silently waited my turn, hidden and still as a shadow behind a bronze velvet curtain that created the tent's false back.

"Would you like an adjustment?" LuAnn said to a customer, pitching her Lady Ezmeralda voice low and velvety. I resisted a snicker. I listened to the gentle balancing of transaction as the person on the other side of the curtain deliberated, but then the hinges on the teak lounge chair squeaked, and I smelled the cut-rose fragrance of LuAnn's triumph. First catch.

I sometimes wondered if it should bother me that I was an invisible part of the show - a show that was impossible without me. Honestly, I was content behind the curtain. Even if no one saw me, I was still helping them.

When I was sixteen and met LuAnn at a local carnival after running away from my group home, I'd imagined her as the witch with the candy house in the woods, waiting for the innocents to come. When we first teamed up to create our booth, I fancied myself the candy - my strange powers baiting the people in the crowd to come to the tent later.

After nearly five years of working together to hone my power over the emotions of others, I knew LuAnn was actually the candy house, and I was the witch. I didn't exactly call my ability magic, but I knew what I could do wasn't quite human, either.

LuAnn was content to just use my power, but I still hoped to learn why I had it. Everywhere we went, I tried to make it to a library to search for new books and scour the internet, but I'd never found more than speculation. Except for the rumors surrounding Underbelly Circus, I'd never heard of anyone else like me.

No one seemed to have anything like what LuAnn called my "psychic empathy."

"Carlyle!" LuAnn's regular voice was back - softly Southern but laced with aggravation. She was already done with the hypnosis, and I hadn't even noticed. Slipping from behind the curtain, I saw a middle-aged man prone and relaxed on the navy silk-draped chair. To anyone else, he could be sleeping.

However, I smelled the ash and midnight-twisted stench of deep, chronic depression, and I sighed. What a way to start the damn night.

"You seem distracted," LuAnn murmured as I knelt beside the man. She tucked a lock of my white-blond hair behind my ear, but I didn't sense any real care on her. She was a business partner and a decent friend, but nothing more.

I shrugged and delicately touched the man's temple, then the nape of his neck, then the back of his skull, my fingers tingling when I found the tangled nest of emotions and memories and expectations of what life was supposed to be.

I closed my eyes and began to unravel the knot, one black thread of self-loathing at a time.

LuAnn had taught me the self-hypnosis of meditation the first year I lived with her. As I worked, I slipped into the dream-like state that allowed me to cordon off the depression flowing from the man's skin into my fingers. Still, those threads were sticky, and some always got tangled in my head. Starting the nights with my extra bits of stolen happiness made my recovery faster.

Finishing, I hid myself behind the curtain again. LuAnn woke the man, who marveled at his newly-improved outlook.

"So much better than a psychiatrist," he gloated. Unfortunately, the effect would be temporary, which was one reason we did festival work instead of setting up a permanent shop.

As we waited for the next customer, I whispered to LuAnn through the flocked velvet. "I'll be twenty-one next month, you know."

"I do."

"We should go on vacation somewhere. The ocean, maybe." I loved it when we found festivals near the sea, but they were always the most expensive to set up a booth. We'd only been twice.

LuAnn chuckled. "We won't be missing festival season in the mid-west for your birthday. Maybe in the late winter months."

I knew that was a lie. It was always festival season in the mid-west. There was always money to be made. LuAnn and I worked well together, but she cared about me mostly in the capacity of an investment. Of course, I used her, too.

I needed the freedom of the open road. I'd never be happy living in one place, and it was easier to stay safe with a partner to watch your back.

"Underbelly is never at the sea in the summer," I pointed out, feeling stubborn. LuAnn feared the Ringmaster's Underbelly Circus almost as much as I did, but she abided by the philosophy of keeping your enemies close. We tracked the Circus's movements carefully through every town, keeping our travels just beyond his ring of influence.

"Go on, then. Just don't expect to come back and find me waiting for you." LuAnn's threats had changed over the last couple of years - at first she'd just shut me down with the idea of going back to foster care. Now she played on my reluctance to go it alone again.

I sighed, backing down. We both knew I wasn't going

anywhere. Not yet, at least.

Through the evening, we treated eight people, earning four hundred dollars. It was a good first night. As our reputation spread, each following night of the festival would usually double or even triple.

"The crowds are all gone," LuAnn finally said, drawing back the velvet curtain. I blinked up at her, groggy and exhausted after a night of pulling negative threads through the fabric of my brain.

Still, I helped collect the candles, curtains, tent, and chairs. We never left anything out overnight. LuAnn parked our camper trailer at a nearby hotel, in the shadowy back of the parking lot. After changing into a thin sleep shirt and loose shorts, I curled on my narrow mattress to sleep off some of the customers' depression.

Yet even as LuAnn's breathing grew steady, I continued to toss. I kept thinking about the ocean, and how much better it was than the muddy, mid-west river just beyond our trailer.

My brain also kept pulling up the red-haired guy's golden eyes and chiseled body, too - taunting me with something I couldn't have and shouldn't want anyway. Even if this one wasn't a recruiter for the Ringmaster, gorgeous guys had always been nothing but trouble for me.

I crawled out of bed and rummaged in the tiny kitchen, getting my sugar fix from a few spoonfuls of ice cream. Even then, I felt unsettled. I sighed, pushing aside the thick blackout curtain and peering into the darkness outside.

The open road beyond was pulling strongly at me tonight.

Even in a sleeping mid-west town, it was dumb to leave

the trailer and walk at night. I knew better, but suddenly, claustrophobia clamped down on my brain. I felt trapped - by the cramped trailer, by the extra emotions and desire pinging around inside me, even by LuAnn's refusal to take a damn vacation.

Fuck it. I could take a walk if I wanted to. LuAnn would be here when I got back. I didn't want to live my life in fear or in hiding.

I grabbed a pair of flip-flops and a light cardigan, slipped my knife into my pocket just in case, and inched open the trailer door. I squeezed out and breathed in the midsummer night's air.

If I could smell my own emotions, I imagined they would be tinged with a bit of lemon-rind excitement right now.

I wasn't ready to be completely alone again, like the miserable months on the streets before I found LuAnn. I was just really damn tired of profiting from others' depression and stealing joy from old women. I wanted a chance for real joy.

Surely I deserved that much.

Behind the shadowy curtains of the candy house, the witch was dreaming of a life of her own.

This wasn't the night to leave LuAnn; I needed more savings and a real plan. Surely there was no harm in pretending, though. I began to wander the quiet, dark streets, heeding the pull toward the road leading straight out of town.

CHAPTER FIVE

CARLYLE

Up ahead, a narrow suspension bridge spanned the fat river. Two lanes - one for coming and one for going. I imagined going and never coming back, and that gorgeous possibility pulled me from the road and onto the bridge.

It was four in the morning and still dark, except for the splashes of light from each naked bulb welded to the bridge frame. There were no cars on the bridge, but there was a guy, I realized suddenly, snapping from my daydreams.

He was silhouetted in a circle of light, his attention fixated on the black water and muddy riverbank a hundred feet below. I sensed danger and depression on the night air - one warned me away, but the other drew me in.

He needed help.

I slipped deeper into the shadows, although I was close enough to be seen if he looked. My heart pounded, and I hoped he wouldn't look - not yet. I needed to assess the situation first.

He was alone as far as I could see, and there was no car nearby. He was at least my age and tall, with dark, scruffy hair and pale skin. Lean but not thin. Dark jeans and a dark tee, loose enough to be careless but tight enough to show his coiled muscles as he gripped the thick metal railing. The white lights defined his cheekbones and fresh-shaved jaw, as sharp finely crafted as an assassin's blade.

He turned and locked his summer sky-blue eyes on my lavender ones, and all I could see was his jagged edges.

I didn't need to touch him to feel his pain. It vibrated the air on the bridge, drawing me closer like a cord around my heart.

Despair snaked around his chest, squeezing his breath into too-small rations. The emotion was so strong I felt like I could see it, although it wasn't a smell like normal. Instead, my thoughts were consumed by it.

Helping him became all that mattered.

I'd barely realized I was moving until I reached the edge of his circle of light. The bright bulb above seared my brain, and I balked. What the hell was I doing, approaching a stranger on my own at night? LuAnn didn't even know I was gone. How well could I really protect myself, with rusty self-defense skills and a tiny pocketknife? He could even be from Underbelly, for all I knew.

Somehow, none of that spiraling logic changed the fact that I *knew* I could help him - I just needed to get close enough to touch him.

"You're a festival person, yeah? Not from this town." The guy interrupted my thoughts, but despite how close we stood, his voice seemed as far away as the morning light. His light Australian accent pegged him as a traveler, too.

I nodded, edging into the light. "What are you doing?" I asked as he swiveled back to the railing, leaning over it to stare straight down.

"Nice night for a swim," he spat back at me. Before I realized what was happening, he'd grabbed one of the bridge's steel suspension cables and hoisted himself onto the flat handrail. He balanced lightly on its narrow surface. I gasped, and he glared down at me.

The moonlight made him even more beautiful, and I was struck with the idea that not only was he not local, he wasn't quite *human*. My chest tightened, and a bead of sweat slid down my back. I'd always suspected there was more to the world than its surface plainness, and not only because of my unique ability to manipulate emotions and smell a person's feelings on the wind.

It was more like missing something I couldn't quite remember - the idea that a whole other world waited for me somewhere.

Underbelly be damned. If this guy knew anything, I had to learn it.

I stepped closer, wrapping my fingers around the cool metal railing a few inches from his boots. Flecks of peeling blue paint crunched beneath my palms.

"I'm sure there's an easier way down if you want to swim. Jump like that could kill a person." I answered his insinuation, forcing my voice to be casual.

"A person? Yeah, that's the idea. But jumpin's the easiest way," he returned, turning on his toes so he faced the night and the drop. He leaned out into the open air a bit, his hands fisted on the cables. His angry tone had calmed a bit, but the sadness was still there. I wondered what he'd done that might push him so close to ending his life.

"Why?" I asked stupidly. I dealt with depressed people at every festival, but I wasn't practiced in coaxing someone off a ledge. The only other time I'd been face to face with a suicidal person, death had won. I gritted my teeth against that feeling of helplessness - I had to try.

If only I could touch him, maybe I could draw out enough depression to get him some real help.

"Why not?" he said with a humorless laugh. "Life. Death. Whatever. It's all the same to me." His voice was haunted with the kinds of demons I hoped I'd never see.

"Well, if it's all the same, then why don't you just live a while longer," I said, fighting to keep my voice steady.

He turned and looked down at me. He even bent his knees, crouching on the railing with one hand still clutching the cable. He rubbed at a thick, plain band of gold on his thumb.

"Here, I'll help you down." I offered my hand up to him. If I could just touch him...

He grasped my hand, and I smiled in encouragement. I could do this.

"What good logic," he growled, gripping my fingers. His anger had returned, but at least now he was closer to me than to the empty nothingness at his back.

Suddenly, I caught the burnt toast stench of a lie. His eyes narrowed, and the air flared with a complex scent that locked my lungs up tight in memory. *Duplicity.*

"No," I whispered, but it was too late.

Tightening his hold on my fingers, he yanked me up onto the railing with him like I weighed nothing. Panicking, I wrapped my arms tight around his lean waist, my feet scrabbling for purchase on the railing. One flip-flop slipped off my toes and floated down, down into the blackness below.

Fucking *hell.* What had I gotten myself into? If he let go now, I'd be going with him.

"Step right up," he murmured against my hair, his arm like a hot iron band around my waist, pressing my body roughly against the ridges of his hard muscle.

My toes found just enough railing that I could stand and focus on calming myself, although I kept my arms locked around him. If it hadn't been such a life-or-death deal, I would have enjoyed this position.

A few of my fingers pushed beneath his shirt, finding the smooth, hot skin of his lower back.

The musty, wet wood smell of regret swirled around us, and something told me he didn't really want to be doing this.

I tried to push into his emotions through my touch, my power hurriedly searching for the tendrils of despair that would have him balancing on a bridge railing in the middle of the night. I dug my fingers into his spine, trying desperately to focus enough to at least push some of my own stolen happiness into him.

There just wasn't enough of my power left - not after a full night's work.

He let go of my waist and reached around to pry my fingers away.

"Fuck, you're strong," he grunted, pulling my arm away and twisting it behind my back. I clung to him with my other hand, too afraid to do anything but hold on. My head spun with the irony: I'd never felt weaker or more helpless.

He laughed without humor, the sound low and grumbly in my ear. "But you can't push your emotions on me."

"What?" I startled against him, uncertain how he could know what I could do. Dread crept into my veins, icing my joints into stiffness. The Ringmaster knew what I could do. This guy really could be working for the Underbelly Circus. My heart hammered - I'd been so stupid.

"I'm immune to your power. You can't manipulate my feelings."

A stab of hope cut through my panic - he *did* know something. I knew I needed to free myself somehow, but maybe this could also be the break I'd been waiting for. If he really was from Underbelly, he wasn't going to throw me to my death.

"Wh-why?" I stammered. "What are you?"

"What are *you*?" he countered, and I snapped my mouth shut and shook my head. That was the problem - I had no idea.

"I know what you are," he whispered into my hair, letting my wrist go and sliding his arm back to my hips. An electric shiver coursed through my body. Instantly, his grasp felt less like a trap and more like a caress, and the lean muscles pressed against me were sensual instead of threatening. I imagined running my fingers along his strong jaw, then maybe my tongue.

The summer night's air scorched between us, and

something deep in my belly clenched with desire.

It was the same sort of primal desire that had once driven me out of my group home and onto the streets at sixteen, where I spent every second running from my own wants until I finally learned to control them.

Now, that control was shattering all around me.

His full lips parted as he chuckled, and the vibrations of his chest against my breasts drew something from my mouth that sounded embarrassingly like a growl of need. I gritted my teeth and swallowed down the noise.

"Ah, fuck," he hissed, his eyes fluttering closed for a second. With a shock, I realized I could feel his cock growing hard between us. "I feel it, too. You're so goddamn strong," he said again. "But you're afraid," he added, a note of wonder in his low voice. His fingers slipped beneath my thin shirt, hot on my lower back.

I tipped my head back to peer at him, my eyes rolling with the dizziness of black river below and black sky above. The stars spun as his eyes glittered, their bright blue unnatural against the black and white around them. I managed to whisper, "Obviously, you idiot. I don't want to die."

"You're not afraid of me," he added, his voice lifting at the end as though it were a question.

"No." The word slipped out, and I realized it might be shit-cake crazy, but it was true. "You just need someone to help you."

For a shadow of a second, I smelled his surprise - the softest brush of crushed mint.

"You *should* be afraid of me," he whispered, and his eyes glinted like fiery jewels. His hand released my waist, and I scrambled for the cable, letting go of him to stabilize myself better.

He was right. I should be afraid of him, but it didn't change the fact that I just wasn't.

"I'd like to see you again," he said, bending over me, fingers pressing against my spine. I shivered as his lips brushed the shell of my ear. "Don't let me down."

Twisting away from me, he jumped before I could even scream.

His beautiful, sad blue eyes stayed locked on mine until the darkness claimed him. I couldn't see the muddy river below, but I heard the wet smack of his body hitting the riverbank. At the sound, my memory ripped open, spilling dark memories of someone else I hadn't been able to save.

I gagged and heaved out a ragged breath that ended on a sob. What the absolute fuck had just happened?

CHAPTER SIX

KILLIAN

I stood in front of the gas station's refrigerated section and rumpled my bright red hair. This night had really gone to shit.

The girl was out there somewhere, so close I could feel her in my bones. I'd lost her in the crush of the crowd, and fuck if I could find her again. I cursed myself for the millionth time for hesitating earlier.

We hadn't had a lead this strong in… ever. I grimaced, thinking about how long we'd been hammering at this search, with only shit to show. No way in fuck was I going to be the one who came so close only to lose it.

I finally grabbed a sugary energy drink and popped open the top, grimacing at the taste. A chemical shit storm only a human would love. Tossing a five onto the counter, I swiped through my limited cell contacts until I found the number for the safe house.

Jai answered on the third ring, just as I pushed back into the muggy summer night.

"Talk, Kills," Jai commanded, stress tightening his voice.

The order made me want to mouth off. Why else would I call, if not to fucking talk? But Jai was obviously in the middle of something, so I just shoved in, balls deep.

"I found her." I gloated that, after all these years, I'd been the one to pick up the trail of our mystery girl.

"How do you know it was her?" Jai asked, cynicism and years of disappointment still not masking the single note of hope that kept us all grinding away at the world's most impossible mission.

"Let's just say, if she's not a Qilin, then we have the wrong intel. You'd know, too, if you saw her." I would never forget that glimpse of pure light radiating from the shadows as she stood beneath that huge tree. Her pale, perfect skin and that wild mane of white-blond hair. Her wide purple eyes, and the way she'd held my challenge stare long enough to pull my dick to attention at fifty yards.

I'd hated it and loved it, all wrapped up in one big goddamn mindfuck.

"How long until you get here?" Jai asked, interrupting a really damn good daydream.

Ah, shit. The fun part was over. "Well, I donna have her with me just yet. I came across a little snag."

"Kills," he warned.

"She's not alone, and you're not going to fuckin'

believe who's here."

"If you say the Ringmaster, I will tear that limp dick right-"

"The Ringmaster." I snickered and held the phone away as Jai unleashed a string of cursing so foul I nearly blushed, which was saying a goddamn lot. Jai was so fun to play with. "I saw Jack!" I yelled into the phone, hoping it would break through Jai's tirade.

The line went silent then, so complete that I actually checked the display to see if the call had dropped. Nope. Our fearless leader, who always knew what to do and say, had been stunned into silence.

"This is where you say, 'good stuff, Killian'," I deadpanned, shoving down the worry that was creeping up my throat like bile. Our team had been separated way too long, and the promise of finding not only the girl but Jack, too, probably had Jai blowing his wad all over the room.

I couldn't fucking screw this up, or we might never get her. Without her, we'd never get home.

"Send me your coordinates. Sol just checked in yesterday - I'll put him on the next flight," Jai finally said, his voice locked down tight again.

"Nah, that's the kick in the nuts. I'm only a few hours' drive from the safe house," I said and rattled off the information Sol would need to find me. "And Jai? Warn him - something's not right with Jack."

CARLYLE

I scrambled off the bridge railing and kicked off my other flip-flop, then began running the length of the grassy shoulder, cursing and looking desperately for a way down to the riverbank. I had to get help, but I had no phone, and I didn't know where anything in this sorry-ass town was.

He was dead.

He had to be, from a fall like that. I couldn't just *leave* him, though.

The brush was dense, though, and by the time I found a passable gap, I was pretty far from the bridge. Slipping and sliding down the hill, I tried to determine where he might have landed when he jumped.

No matter how many times I looked up at the bridge and tried to judge the trajectory, I couldn't find a fucking thing on the dark ground before me.

My stomach sickened with the thought that maybe he'd rolled into the dark water.

Falling to my bare knees in the foul river mud, I dry-heaved, choking on sobs. I didn't even know this guy, but his loss practically paralyzed me. It was such a senseless act, and I'd done nothing to help him. Me - who made my living helping people.

Sure, it was sort of an act, but it satisfied something deep inside me, too. I did what I could to make this shitty world a better place.

Now, I'd watched someone die again, and I didn't even know his name. I couldn't even find someone who might know him or care about him. My emotions bottomed out, and dizziness sucked all the energy from my limbs.

In my heart, I knew it wasn't my fault. That didn't stop the guilt tumbling over me in waves, sucking me under like a riptide.

I fought against it, knowing I couldn't stay here in the

mud. I had to get back to LuAnn, and I'd have to figure out how to deal with this.

This night would haunt me forever, too.

Hugging my arms to my waist, I stumbled up the hill in a daze, ignoring the scratch of weeds against my battered feet and ankles. Dawn had broken, and as I padded barefoot down the road, I watched the purple-hazed bruise of early morning creep across the sky.

I trudged into the parking lot, my heart and head aching as I picked my way over the loose gravel.

As I neared LuAnn's trailer, though, I heard voices from the other side, where the door was.

"Who are you and what do you want with the girl?" LuAnn demanded.

I froze. She had to be talking about me. Maybe someone had seen what happened on the bridge and called the cops to investigate. My first instinct was to run, to bolt out of the parking lot. Something made me hesitate, though. I needed to know more about who was looking for me.

"I've come to offer you a deal," a hard, flat male voice said. I could almost hear the cruel smile in his words, and I shivered. This was no cop. I stepped closer, pressing myself to the side of the trailer until I could peek around the edge.

LuAnn's back was to me, and whoever she was talking to was mostly hidden from view.

She squared her shoulders. "I don't deal with anyone except customers."

"The Ringmaster sent me," he said, and my knees nearly gave out. Fuck. Fuck, fuck, *fuck*. This was bad. Was it the redhead? I couldn't see without giving myself away.

41

I'd never seen the Ringmaster himself, either, but I still feared him more than anything else in the world. The Underbelly Circus was the one circus a performer never joined out of choice, and never left alive.

I'd dodged him twice. Was third time a charm for him or me?

A rotten, earthy scent of fear surged from LuAnn. I knew I should run, but I had no idea where to go this time. I didn't have any money on me. Hell, I didn't even have shoes. My brain spun its wheels while my body stayed frozen.

"Underbelly wants *her.*"

Suddenly, a finger was pointing in my face. My eyes grew so wide they should have fallen out of my goddamn head.

Right in front of me, grinning in triumph, was the dude from the motherfucking bridge. No broken bones. No split flesh.

He wasn't even fucking muddy!

My mouth flopped open and closed like a fish, words refusing to come as anger surged through me. To think I'd wasted hours trying to help this asshole!

"The Ringmaster sent me to find and collect her." His accent crept back in, though his eyes were carefully blank. He turned back to LuAnn, offering her a crisp white envelope from his back pocket. "This is for you. Get out of here before it expires and trouble finds you."

LuAnn's fingers shook as she took the envelope. Her eyes flickered to mine, and I could see the terror in them. The scent of cowardice exploded into my nostrils like the squish of a boot in dank mud, and I knew.

She was going to let this guy take me.

She was going to abandon me to some freak show and likely an early grave.

In that moment, I realized I'd depended on LuAnn too fucking long, and I'd gone soft and lazy. She was a bitch, for sure, but I had no one to blame but myself now. It was time for me to take charge of my own life again.

Adrenaline shot through my body. My muscles unlocked, and I bolted. Sprinting across the gravel, I cried out against the sharp pain in my tender feet, but I kept running.

Footsteps pounded behind me. Just as I reached the grass again, I was tackled from behind and rolled to my back on the ground. The asshole straddled my hips, his blue eyes blank and his expression stoic as he stared down at me.

"I'm sorry it had to be this way, but we've been waiting a long time for one like you."

"Get off! Let me go," I yelled, hitting and kicking and clawing at him. He was too strong. He blocked my out-of-practice blows with comical ease, waiting for me to tire. I kept screaming, praying someone would overhear. Why was there no one around?

Then an engine rumbled to life, and a sob fought its way from my chest. Over the guy's shoulder, I could just glimpse LuAnn's stricken face as she peeled out of the parking lot.

The trailer rattling out of sight paralyzed me just long enough for exhaustion to overpower the adrenaline, and I collapsed back on the ground, the back of my head thudding into the grass.

I was too weak to fight him when he lifted his weight from me and gently pulled me up. A wave of dizziness overpowered me, and I slumped against him as he brushed grass and leaves from me. Damn him for being so fucking gentle.

I concentrated first on shutting down my emotions one by one, as I'd done once before, years ago.

I needed to gather my energy and evaluate my options. Was now the time to survive, not run?

His movements robotic, the guy tugged me toward a nondescript brown car, and I stumbled after him. As he nudged me closer, though, hot shame trickled down my spine that I wasn't fighting this. Fuck surviving - if I didn't fight now, I might not have the chance again.

Heart pounding, I scraped together enough energy to yank free of his grasp again. I only made it a few steps before he caught my long hair in his fist.

I cried out and barely had a chance to break my fall as I dropped to my bare knees in the gravel. My scalp throbbed as he twisted his handful of hair.

He reached back and opened the car door with his other hand, then let go of my hair to hook both arms under mine. He hauled me backward, aiming to shove me in the open car. I skidded on the loose pebbles, struggling to break free.

Just before he forced me in, though, a silver sports car screeched into the parking lot. It slammed straight into the brown one, knocking it sideways. My head smashed against the edge of the door, and I tumbled to my hands and knees again, moaning.

Two huge guys burst from the silver car, shouting at the Underbelly guy.

I scuttled away from the wheels, my head throbbing and my skin stinging with a thousand tiny cuts.

Behind me, the three of them burst into a tornado of flying fists and kicks, a whirlwind of color and shouts. I dragged myself toward the grass, but the extreme emotional and physical demands of the night bowled me over until all I could do was wonder what the fuck I was seeing.

Hallucinations, obviously. I'd hit my head pretty damn hard.

Bursts of light like movie magic streaked the early morning sky. A fierce golden lion roared and leaped onto the brown car, claws carving deep grooves in the metal. And then, of all things, an enormous, garnet-colored dragon shot into the sky, spiraling away until it disappeared into the orange and pink sunrise.

My mind cracked open, my sanity leaking onto the ground all around me. My eyes slid closed in pain, exhaustion claimed my thoughts, and I dropped into oblivion.

CHAPTER SEVEN

CARLYLE

I woke with a burst of nervous energy, flinging myself out of bed. My feet hit plush carpet, not splinter-laden plywood. My bare legs turned to goose-flesh at the unfamiliar chill of serious air-conditioning, and I shivered beneath the oversized t-shirt I wore.

Wait.

Not my bed, not my corner of LuAnn's trailer. Not even my shirt. Where the hell was I? Had the Ringmaster gotten me after all? I couldn't remember, and it was freaking me the fuck out.

Working to calm my breathing, I forced myself to examine the space around me for clues. It was messy and masculine, but it was an actual *room*. Like in a house - not a hotel or circus trailer.

Flashes of the night before started lighting up in my mind, like a car's headlights illuminating one thing at a time. The guy on the bridge. Make that the *asshole* on the bridge.

Oh, and then LuAnn leaving me behind - fucking bitch. The reality of her abandonment knocked me back physically, and I slumped onto the bed, my stomach rolling.

Her betrayal didn't surprise me, though. Not really.

No pity parties here, but eventually, everyone in my life sold me out. Five years with LuAnn was longer than I'd stayed anywhere. I'd felt the end coming, and I'd stupidly ignored it. No more, though. I nodded to myself, feeling instantly stronger as I made the decision to strike out alone again. I could survive on my own - I'd done it before LuAnn, after all.

First, I'd figure out where the hell I was, and where I could go from here. I reasoned that if I wasn't in Underbelly right now, and I obviously wasn't in a hospital or a jail, then most likely the two latecomers in the silver car had grabbed me up.

The ones with the... lion.

My brain sputtered out there as I recalled my hallucinations of magical sparks, giant animals, and mystical creatures. Nope. I really shouldn't trust whoever had brought me here, either. Maybe I'd been drugged somehow.

I was missing some important chunks of memory from the night before.

I scoured the room for my own clothes, but all I found were men's clothes - all casual and amazingly soft, but way too large. I slipped into a pair of track pants, but even after rolling the waist several times, they still dragged the floor. Still, saggy pants were an improvement over no pants.

Seriously, who undresses a stranger while she's unconscious? A douchebag, that's who.

I was checking for sneakers or flip flops - anything I could wear without tripping - when the door flung open.

"She's up!" The guy filling the doorway was oddly familiar. He turned his face back to mine after yelling to someone else, and I gasped when it hit me. Those golden eyes - I definitely wouldn't forget that iron grip of a stare.

I also recalled his flaming hair, which was delightfully messy and spiky on top and crept down his jawline in the yummiest bronze stubble ever. My fingers curled against themselves as I imagined scratching my nails along that gorgeous jawline, and - wait.

I struggled to curb my flash of desire. Totally uncalled-for. This guy was basically a kidnapper. He'd been following me around the day before, and he'd probably been the one who undressed me while I was unconscious. Dick move, even if my clothes had been torn and covered in riverbank mud.

My legs were also wiped clean of mud, too, so….

"What do you want with me?" I demanded, planting my hands on my hips and glaring up at him. Why did he have to be so tall?

He grinned, slow and confident, and the gesture warmed my skin more than I wanted to admit. I took a step back, wishing I could back away from my own damned desire, too.

The back of my knees bumped against the bed, and I bit the inside of my cheek.

"I want a lot o' things. Donna mean I'll get them," the redhead answered, his lightly-Irish voice rough as his eyes noted the stolen pants. I crossed my arms over my chest, feeling way too vulnerable.

"Where the fuck am I?" I tried to keep my panic locked up, giving him the bitch treatment instead. I wanted to ask him about Underbelly, but I was afraid to hear the answer. "And how did I get here, and fucking why?"

He chuckled. "Not surprised you donna remember. You were pretty cracked last night."

"Cracked? Did you give me something? Drugs?" So much for controlling my panic. I took a few deep breaths. Whatever they wanted, I would handle it. I would find a way out. I would fight for my freedom like I always had.

The redhead only chuckled at my accusation. "Sol!" he yelled over his shoulder, then turned back to me. "No. We've not given you anythin' but a safe place to sleep."

"Underbelly," I whispered. Was it too naive to hope his claim meant they were keeping me safe from those horrific rumors?

"They won't fuckin' get ya." His eyes darkened to an amber flame, sparking across the room at me. My knees buckled in relief and surprise at his sudden ferocity, and I sank into the soft mattress behind me.

Before either of us could speak another word, the redhead was pushed aside as another unreasonably tall guy made his way into the room.

"Wow," he said, lifting an eyebrow at the redhead. "You were right. Seems you have some use after all, Kills," he complimented the other man. He had tangled, dark blond waves gathered at the back of his neck in a loose bundle, and he was just as beautiful as the redhead, with

49

full, Cupid's bow lips and deep chocolate eyes.

I clenched my teeth as need pooled in my core.

Fuck this. I'd worked for years to master my dangerous urges to, ah, get busy. I was never tempted to run off with random guys anymore - it had been a couple of years since I'd even kissed anyone, and I was goddamn proud of that.

Then three guys in two days had shattered every inch of control I had over my wayward thoughts.

"Right about what?" I drew my legs onto the bed and scooted to its other side, hitching up the saggy ass of my borrowed pants. The two men were blocking the only way out of this room, but at least I could put some space between us. I needed to figure this weirdness out, ASAP.

"We've been searching for someone with your, uh, abilities. For a really long time," Blondie said, pausing to take a long drink from a steaming mug.

Coffee. I groaned, the scent of hazelnut roast filling my nose.

Wait. Why wasn't I smelling their emotions? I should be able to read both of them.

Now that I was concentrating, it was obvious how blank they were. I smelled the clean laundry scent of the shirt I was wearing and the rich aroma of the coffee, but these were normal smells. Anyone could smell them.

Problem was, I wasn't just anyone when it came to scents.

My nerves thrummed as I stacked up what I knew. My power over emotions hadn't worked on the bridge last night. Now, I couldn't smell emotions from these two. It had to be related, which meant these guys could still be tied to the Circus.

Fear sliced through my limbs, and I scrambled off the back of the bed, scanning more insistently for a way out of the room.

No matter what these guys wanted, they'd somehow voided out the only advantage I'd ever had on the world, and that was bad.

"We're scaring her," Blondie said to Kills, his deep voice soft and rumbly. "Sweetheart, we're the good guys."

I snorted a panicked laugh. That's what the bad guys always claimed, right? "What the hell kind of good guy is named Kills? I really need some answers now."

"Or what?" Kills asked, smirking. Blondie elbowed him hard in the gut, and he grunted. "Fine. I'm Killian, and this cheap shot is Solomon. We really have been lookin' for ya."

"Why?" I asked, keeping an eye on the door.

"It's Sol," Blondie corrected, shoving Killian against the door frame. "And that's a long story." He raked back a golden strand that had come free of its tie. "We're really supposed to wait until Jai gets here and has final say on who you are. He's our team leader."

I narrowed my eyes. Who did they think I was? I was just another runaway-turned-carnie. Nobody. "Team what?"

"Team you," Sol said, meeting my eyes with a shy smile. Although it sounded like a cheesy line, I sensed the truth there. It didn't have a smell, exactly, but it was in his open face and kind eyes. Deep, dark chocolate eyes. Ugh. He was so hot, it just wasn't playing fair.

"Relax, kid," Killian said, rolling his eyes as though he could sense my fractured thoughts. "You'll not be hurt here." He turned and swaggered away from the doorway, leaving me staring at the mountain named Sol and biting back a retort about not being a kid.

CHAPTER EIGHT

CARLYLE

"So, do you want some?" Sol asked, stepping toward me. My brain short-circuited as I stared at him. Hell yes, I wanted some. I wanted to jump off the bed and climb him. His skin was like golden honey, and I wanted to lap up its sweet-

He shook the empty mug in my face. "Coffee. Do you want some?" he repeated.

I felt my whole body flush in embarrassment. Ah. Of course, he was talking about coffee.

For the love of all things sugar, I needed to get a grip.

I'd gone from worrying about being drugged and kidnapped by strangers to imagining both of them in bed with me.

Wait. Did I say both? Ah, *shit*.

I shook my head like an animal, trying to clear the fog. "Um, yes. Coffee would be fantastic. Thank you," I added.

Sol backed out of the room, keeping his eyes solidly on me, like maybe I was a threat or something.

Maybe he thought I would run. Part of me wanted to, sure, but I still didn't have anywhere to go. Still didn't have money. Still didn't have any goddamn shoes.

"I really need some answers," I told him again as I followed him down the bare hallway. I felt my eyes go all pleading, like a baby animal, and I ducked my head so he wouldn't see it. I refused to break down. I'd never been a crier, and I wasn't about to start now.

He glanced back, his gaze sweeping down my body. A tiny smile quirked up the corners of his mouth, coaxing a dimple into his cheek. Of course, he would have a dimple. "I won't let anything happen to you," he said.

I padded behind him into the kitchen without a word. No one had ever said that to me before, and certainly no one had ever assumed that kind of responsibility for me. I wished I could trust it, but I just didn't.

I leaned against the dark-wood kitchen table while he poured the coffee, reminding myself not to get comfortable, because I wouldn't be here long. I tried not to ogle the way his biceps bunched up at the simple motion of lifting a coffee pot. Instead, I noted the bare counters and lack of decoration - it was like they hadn't lived here long at all.

"Cream and sugar?" he asked, and I nodded.

"Sugar makes everything better," I said, feeling my face flush again at his answering grin. I took the mug and the offered sugar bowl, dumping several spoonfuls in before taking a huge gulp of sweet caffeine. It burned going down, but it tasted so good, I didn't even care.

"So, what do you remember from last night?" Sol asked, sliding into a seat. I stared down into my mug, wondering how much of what I remembered had actually happened. He kicked a chair out for me, and I stared down at it for a second before giving in and plonking into the seat.

I wasn't sure I could talk about all that shit without dropping my coffee.

"I think... I'm not sure what I saw, really. The guy on the bridge - Jack? I don't know how he survived."

"You saw him before the parking lot?" he questioned, raising his brows. "Jack," he repeated.

I nodded. "I went for a walk. It was late, and it was stupid, I know. I just needed to get out for a bit."

Killian sidled into the room and leaned against the doorway with his hands tucked in his pockets, watching me with those sharp golden eyes.

I took a deep breath, desperately wishing I could scent their emotions. That part of my ability had always been my shield - my warning system. Without it, I wasn't sure who I could trust.

"I saw someone on the bridge, and then he climbed up on the railing. I wanted to help him. He was so sad." My voice trailed away, remembering the paralyzing depression I'd sensed on him - before he'd turned into the world's biggest prick.

"How did you know he was sad?" Killian asked. I blinked up at him.

"Just his eyes," I said, and his face grew hard, like he'd recognized the lie. I rushed on with my story. "When I went to talk to him, he pulled me up with him. I just knew I was going over, too. Then I thought he was getting down, and then he jumped! I heard his body hit the mud," I whispered, trying to shut down the wet smack in my memory. It was the second suicide I'd witnessed - the second person I'd failed to help.

Sol reached across the table, his long fingers closing around my clenched fist, and the air blossomed with a heady summer scent, like fields of warm grass and damp earth with a hint of honeysuckle. My traitorous stomach bottomed out with need, and I snatched my hand back, my eyes wide as I stared at him.

The scents vanished, leaving just the smell of sugary coffee.

What the crap? This was so not the time for my power to be on the fritz. I pulled my long hair over my shoulder and began to braid it, giving my shaking hands something to do.

"Was there anything else?" Killian asked, rummaging in the fridge for something, oblivious to the intense staring session between Sol and me. "Did he say anything weird to you?" His tone was a bit too casual, and I broke my gaze with Sol to study Killian as he turned around, shoving a whole slice of cheese in his mouth.

"He said 'I'd like to see you again'," I blurted. Ugh, that *jerk*. He'd known exactly what he was doing. If I did ever see him again, I was going to push some serious karma straight into his soul.

Then I remembered the other odd things he'd said. He'd called me strong when I obviously wasn't. He'd known about my ability to manipulate emotions, which was almost certainly what the Ringmaster wanted to add to his collection of freaks.

If I wasn't so terrified of Underbelly, it would have been the logical place to go for answers about myself. It was probably how they caught so many people in the first place.

"What is it?" Sol asked, the concern in his deep, gravelly voice grasping something deep in my core and squeezing.

I took another large swallow of coffee to compose myself, and he fastened his gaze on me again, his full lips pressed together in worry. My tongue darted out to moisten my lips, and his expression went from flat to fire in the blink of an eye.

Ah, shit. He'd seen my desire and raised it, like a goddamn devastating game of poker. I edged my chair back, feeling more and more like prey. His eyes followed my movements, his bulk sinuous and patient, like a lion stalking an antelope.

That would be me. The skittish meal this guy wanted to devour - slowly, by the glint in his deep brown eyes.

Too many tense seconds of silence passed, and I was again lost inside a fuck or fight stare-down. Except this time, I couldn't find the self-preservation to back down. Something like a low growl made its way from Sol's chest, and the table he was leaning against seemed to vibrate against my fingers.

"Look away, kiddo," Killian whispered, edging behind Sol and toward me, his hands out like he might have to fight his friend. "Sol's losing his cool. He doesn't bite in his human form, but you shouldna play with a caged animal."

"Human form?" I managed, the words squeaking out

like the mew of a terrified kitten. Sol's head swiveled to Killian, and I was able to breathe again. When he turned back to me, he seemed more relaxed. Still, I kept my gaze just over his left shoulder, somewhere between the two guys.

"I'm a shifter," Sol said then, tilting his head at me in confusion. "I thought you saw me last night." He raised his brows as I gaped at him. "You can't tell, can you?"

"Tell?" I repeated, feeling stupid. Hysterical laughter bubbled up in my chest, and I bit it back. I had a feeling my whole world had changed in the space of a night, and as much as I'd wanted it to, I was so not ready.

Sol glanced again at Killian, eyes narrowed. "She doesn't know," he said, his voice a mix of wonder and fury.

"What? What don't I know?" I demanded, a feeling of dread creeping up my spine.

Killian sighed. "Shit. You donna seem to know anythin'."

CHAPTER NINE

KILLIAN

"I'm sorry everything happened like this," Sol spoke up, and I was grateful at least one of us could be calm here, because I was about to lose my motherfucking shit. Who had kept this girl so goddamn sheltered that she didn't even recognize her own kind?

Where was her fucking Qilin mother in all of this?

Sol continued, "We've been waiting a long time. Searching for you a long time. We just never thought you'd know so little about it all."

I struggled to hold back my rage, because I could tell she thought it was directed at her. She'd scooted closer to Sol and kept watching me out of the corner of her eye, like she was afraid of me.

I just couldn't believe she'd lived her whole goddamn life not knowing what she was.

Not knowing what any of us were, evidently.

We were about to rock her world, and not a second of it was going to be fun. Fuck, I hated being in a position like this.

I grabbed the butter, more cheese, and bread, making myself busy with the stove. I'd heard Qilin liked sweets, but we didn't keep that stuff around. In my experience, though, grilled cheese solved a lot.

Sol said, "Jai should be here in a couple hours. He knows the most. But we can give you the basics." The girl clutched her mug tightly, her cheeks pink, those dark purple-blue eyes cast down to the table. Her long hair was already falling out of the loose braid she'd tried to make. My fingers itched to comb through it like I had last night, trying to clean the crusted blood from her temple.

Fucking Jack. I bit down on a snarl, but the frying pan hit the stove a little too hard, and she jumped.

Sol lowered his voice to a more soothing tone and continued, "The world you live in isn't the only world there is. All the stories you've probably heard - vampires, werewolves, fae, whatever. They're all bastardized versions of some race on our world, Haret. A long time ago, travel between the two worlds was easy enough for the right people and the right price. Then someone got greedy, and everything was ruined. Now, we're stuck here unless we find transport home."

Okay, so Sol was a shit storyteller.

But I wasn't about to get in the middle of this - not unless I had to. I set a hot sandwich in front of the girl, stepping away quickly, but not fast enough to escape her moan of pleasure as she inhaled the buttery goodness. I gulped and busied myself making another sandwich.

"So…," Sol said.

I smirked at Sol's distraction, but fuck if I was any better. My back to the table, I tried to discreetly adjust myself. Problem was, there wasn't much discreet about fae dick. I hated that the girl had so much power over me.

It was fucking indecent, really.

"This all sounds impossible," she muttered. She picked the crust off her sandwich like a little kid, then shoved a huge bite of the cheesy middle in her mouth.

"Anything is possible," I said, glancing back at her. "Look at you, right? You steal emotions from one person and give them to someone else. Like some crazy Robin Hood of mind games."

She nearly choked on her food, her eyes growing round. Gulping down more coffee, she stared up at me. "How do you know that?"

I shrugged. "You're a Qilin, kiddo. It's what they do. Or one thing, anyway." I bit back a grin as she scowled at the nickname.

Sol shot me a glare. "I thought we were going slow here."

"This is me going slow, *shifter*," I said, drawing out the last word to point out that he'd need to man up and explain it soon enough. She'd seen Sol last night, even if she wasn't ready to believe it. My phone vibrated, and I fished it out of my jeans pocket. "Jai should be here-" I started, but the words halted as I actually read the text from our team leader.

GET OUT NOW. COMPROMISED.

Ah, fuck.

"Move, Sol," I ordered, my voice brooking no argument. Sol surged up from the table, grabbing the girl's hand as she shrieked. Her coffee mug rolled off the edge of the table and shattered. "We have to get out of this house," I yelled at her as she fought Sol to get free. I snatched my keys from the counter.

Thankfully, Sol hauled her into a bear hug over the broken pieces of mug, and they sprinted after me for the car in the driveway.

Seconds after we screeched away from the curb, the safe house exploded like something off a goddamn action movie set.

The girl screamed and ducked farther into Sol's lap, her face damn near on lion boy's dick. I cursed the lucky fucker while I took corners on two wheels, zooming out of the suburban neighborhood.

A huge shadow passed above us. I slammed my fist against the steering wheel and my foot against the accelerator, my poor beautiful car tearing toward the highway on two wheels. Jack was up there, and he was a deadly motherfucker.

My rage doubled as I owned up to the fact that Jack must have been seriously fucked up by that circus - this was so much worse than going rogue.

I had no idea how Jack had been compromised, but our teammate was definitely no longer one of us.

CARLYLE

What was my life, seriously?

I was going to die of a heart attack before I even

turned twenty-one. I was on my stomach, stretched awkwardly across Sol's huge body. My toes barely scraped the floorboard, and I buried my face deep in Sol's chest, clinging to his biceps for dear life as Killian drove like he planned to kill us all.

Sol's arm was a band of heat around my waist, though, and despite knowing I could die any second, I understood he would do anything possible to prevent it.

Killian kept up a steady stream of cursing as he weaved through traffic, leaning all the way forward to peer up in the sky. We were nowhere near the tiny town from the previous night, and this scared me as much as his crazy driving and the fact that the guys' safe house had just been blown up.

My old life with LuAnn was officially gone, but I had yet to see if being with Killian and Sol was really any fucking better than being dragged into the Underbelly world.

The car swerved into a low-ceilinged tunnel, and darkness draped over us as Killian slowed enough for me to catch my breath.

"He can't fit in here," Killian said, dimming his lights. No other cars were even on the road here.

"He'll be waiting on the other side, though," Sol said. "How the fuck did Underbelly get him?"

The question didn't seem to be directed at anyone, and I certainly had no answers. "So Jack the asshole hasn't always worked for the Ringmaster?" I asked, twisting into a sitting position. Damn, my back was sore now. Of course the stupid, pretty car had no back seat.

Sol grunted softly as I shifted in his lap, trying to get more comfortable. Killian snickered as I reached back and stretched the seatbelt over both of us. I glared back at him, and his golden eyes flashed in the semi-darkness.

Both guys stayed quiet for a long beat. "No," Sol finally said, his palm coming to rest on my thigh. "Jack's one of us."

"He was," Killian corrected, his voice dark and furious. "This is more than going rogue."

"He is," Sol insisted, his voice low and lethal. "Something's wrong, though. Jack would never defect."

His voice was hard with certainty, and somehow I knew if Jack had switched sides out of choice, it would destroy Sol.

Sol rolled down his window and took a deep breath of the tunnel's dank air. "I don't smell him anymore."

Killian nodded, and the car shot out of the tunnel, swerving between lanes as he pushed it to the max.

Ignoring dignity completely, I curled into myself and buried my face in Sol's neck, praying I would make it out of this car alive. Sol held me tightly, his fingers splayed across my spine, stroking up and down a few inches at a time.

I kept my eyes squeezed shut, focusing hard on his summery scent and the calming motion of his touch, not the queasiness of my stomach from Killian's insane driving.

CHAPTER TEN

CARLYLE

After what seemed like a million years, the car began to slow, and finally we came to a stop under a wide bridge. Both men leaned forward to scan the skies carefully, relaxing when they evidently didn't see any further threat.

Before either of them could stop me, I unclicked the seatbelt and yanked on the door handle. I couldn't stand another second in this car.

I practically tumbled onto the roadside. Sol and Killian climbed out and stretched in the relative safety of the shade. Sol's soft t-shirt rode up over the low waistband of his worn jeans, and my gaze skipped across his lower abs and that lovely vee of his muscles. Killian scratched his chest and yawned.

I had no clue how they were so casual after everything that had gone down in the last twelve hours.

"Okay, I appreciate the effort to keep me safe, but I really need more answers than this. I don't know where I am, or who you really are. And I still have no fucking shoes!"

Killian snickered, rolling his eyes as I hoisted up the huge pants and re-rolled them.

Something between a scream and a growl made its way past my clenched teeth, and he backed up a step. So he had a bit of self-preservation, after all. I breathed in deeply several times, pulling my tangled heap of hair over my shoulder again to braid. The action calmed me a little, giving that illusion of control.

There was nothing to be done about my ill-fitting clothes or the fact that I could use a shower. Nothing would change that I was still starving after my breakfast had been blown up. The only thing I had control over was the fact that I wasn't fucking moving from under this bridge until they gave me more information.

"First of all, what is a chee-" I paused, trying to remember the word Killian had thrown at me back at the house.

"Q-I-L-I-N," Sol spelled. "*Chee-lin*. A lot of humans call them unicorns."

Annnd that was it. I threw my hands in the air - I wasn't taking this shit anymore. "A unicorn. Are you kidding me right now? I'm a fucking *unicorn*? Look, if you're not going to give me straight answers, then I'm out of here. Someone will pick me up, and I'll manage from there." I started walking, my common sense shattered by his ridiculous answer.

I got seven steps before Sol caught up. He didn't say a word, just strolled along next to me, angling his huge body to cock block any attempt I might make at hitchhiking.

"What." I refused to look at him, keeping my eyes on the broken roadside. I really needed a pair of goddamn shoes.

"Just making sure you stay safe," he said. "It must be a lot to take in. But haven't you ever wondered about your powers?"

"Of course, I have! I'm not an idiot. I've just never found anything in research, and I've never met anyone like me."

"Because there isn't anyone like you," he said, and I glanced toward him. I was back to being nose-blind, and I had no idea what emotions might be keeping him quiet, his eyes calmly scanning the sky.

"What are you looking for, exactly?" I asked, avoiding the cheesy line.

"Jack. He's a dragon shifter."

"Great. Good to know. Is that what you are, too?" I huffed, picking my way across a patch of gravel. Of course, I had no intention of believing his bullshit.

"No, I'm a lion shifter." He shook his wavy blond hair like it was a goddamn mane or something.

"Oh, awesome. And Killian? Is he, like, a werewolf, or something?" Sarcasm was my best defense today, evidently.

Sol chuckled. "Dare you to ask him that. He's not a shifter. He's a fae."

"Fae. Like a fairy?" For some reason, this one really amused me, and I giggled at the mental image of the tough redhead decked out in glittery wings and tights or whatever the shit fairies wore.

"And your leader?"

"Jai is what you'd probably call a vampire, but it's not much like the movies," Sol said, sliding his eyes to me.

"Oh, don't worry. I'm totally freaking out. It's all just fine," I assured him, hearing the note of mania in my voice and not even caring.

"Please, we really just want to keep you safe." His fingers reached to stroke my bare arm, but he didn't grab me. There was a note of desperation in his voice, and I finally turned to stare at him.

I wasn't exactly on board with all the magical creature stuff, but I took inventory of what I knew, ignoring the fact that I was in a bad place with no home, job, or money. I'd gotten out of that sort of mess once; I could do it again if needed.

It would just be really fucking convenient if Sol and Killian truly were the good guys.

I laid it all out in my head: Jack had definitely been trying to bring me to the Ringmaster. And Jack used to be part of their team. He obviously wasn't on their side anymore, so it made sense that these two didn't want me anywhere near Underbelly Circus.

Sol and Killian *had* kept me safe so far, and they probably had all the answers I'd been searching for my whole life. I sighed - even for a girl who relied exclusively on emotions, the logic here was plain.

"Okay. Let's say I stay with you for a little bit. What's your next step?" The words were hard to form, and turning my steps back toward the sleek silver car was even harder. I didn't trust easily, but I didn't seem to have a lot of choices here.

Despite my anger-induced bravado, it was insanity to walk the highway in nothing but a t-shirt and some baggy men's pants, relying on whoever stopped to do the right thing.

I hadn't survived this long by making stupid decisions. I just needed to control my freaking out better than this.

Sol answered, "When a safe house is compromised, we keep moving. Jai will find a new one and contact us with its location."

"Who are you running from?" I asked. Even if they were the good guys, I would be taking on new enemies by casting my lot with them.

"Underbelly, for one. Mostly we've been searching. Our mission has always been to find you and bring you home to Haret."

"Why me?" That piece was the biggest hurdle in my mind. Compared to dragons and lion shifters and fae, who was I? We were nearly at the car now, and Killian met my glance, his eyes deepening to a sparkling cinnamon hue.

"You're the last Qilin," Killian said. "The only one left who can save Haret from itself." He slid back into the driver's seat.

"Well, fuck," I whispered, and Sol chuckled. I'd never read a lot of teenage fantasy books, namely because I could never stomach the "chosen one" idea. The world was too big for one person to save.

And *two* worlds? I sure hoped these guys had a plan B.

"I'm sorry," Sol said again, seeming to admit the impossibility of what he'd told me. This time, I let myself believe him.

He climbed back in the car, and I settled on his lap, leaning against the hard heat of his chest.

One arm came up behind my shoulders as he closed the car door, curling around me like a pillow. If pillows were made of solid muscle.

Honestly, it could have been a lot worse.

CHAPTER ELEVEN

CARLYLE

Killian kept us on the road until night fell, changing directions randomly as far as I could tell. We stopped only once for greasy hamburgers and a bathroom. Finally, he pulled into a cheap motel and went into the tiny office to pay for a single room. Sol and I untangled ourselves, and I crawled out of the cramped car, rubbing at my stiff muscles.

The room had two beds, but Sol volunteered to sleep on the couch. One look at his gigantic frame compared to the two-cushion couch, though, and I was shaking my head and pointing to the spot next to me.

"I sleep small," I said. I certainly wasn't getting on that nasty-looking couch, but I was fine with sharing. "Like, I don't move around at all. Years of a tiny trailer mattress and nowhere to roll but onto the floor."

Killian grinned, his golden eyes flashing. "After that car ride, I doubt Sol's worried about you rollin' into him tonight. But a deal's a deal - if I get the food, I get a full bed to myself," he warned, slamming out of the door before either of us could answer.

I shrugged and flopped backward across one of the beds - it felt like heaven to stretch out my aching body. I could feel multiple bruises on my knees and arms, plus a few nasty scrapes from hitting the pavement the night before. My head still throbbed when I moved too fast. I probably had a damn concussion.

"How long until we get to a new safe house?" I asked, shucking off the too-big track pants to check my knees. One of the guys must have treated my open cuts the night before, because they were clean and had already scabbed over well enough. I pulled the t-shirt down to cover my thighs and stretched out on my belly.

Sol shook his head, frowning as he flipped channels on the muted television. "Jai can usually get one in place overnight. He's always scouting for options. The fact that it's taken this long has me worried."

I pushed up on my elbows. "Would someone go after Jai? Does the Ringmaster know about all of you?"

"If he has Jack, then maybe. Jack shouldn't break under pressure, but there was something different about him last night. Kills thinks he's been spelled."

"Spelled? Like magic?" Obviously, I was going to have to admit that magic was real. Still, I kinda wanted to ease into the idea.

Sol nodded. "The Ringmaster is a mage, from what

we've seen secondhand. Dair would be able to tell for sure - he's another one of our team."

"Wait." I sat all the way up. "How many are on your team, exactly?"

"Six. Dair and Toro are the ones I hadn't mentioned yet. They're both on separate missions trying to find you, just like Kills and I were. Jack, too," he added. "We've been rotating geographical sections, while Jai combed the internet and monitored everyone's locations."

I blinked at him in disbelief. Six of them, and their sole assignment was to find me?

"We've never had much to go on," Sol said, as if sensing my skepticism. "We didn't even know your name until last night. We've been literally searching the world, country by country and town by town, looking for rumors of someone with Qilin powers or that special look. Finding out about Underbelly was actually a big break at first - we think nearly all the performers are Haretians or mixed human and Haretian."

"Wow," I whispered. Yeah, I could imagine that would be a difficult mission. Especially since LuAnn and I hadn't stayed more than a few nights in the same town for years. I sank back into the starched sheets and pillows. I'd pretty much assumed there was more out there in the world than regular old humanity.

But this? This was all way more involved than I'd ever imagined.

"I'm sorry," Sol said. "This must be a lot to take in."

I waved my hand at him. "I've wanted answers my whole life. I just never expected them to be so complicated." My tone came out a bit harsher than I'd intended, and he turned away, pushing the waxy curtain open to scan the dark parking lot below. Cursing at myself, I scrambled out of bed and padded to him, placing my hand on his forearm. "I'm sorry, Sol. It's a lot to take in, but I don't have to take it out on you."

That sweet, summer-grass aroma of pleasure bloomed from his skin, marking the second time I could smell his emotions. Why wasn't it all the time, though?

"That woman who left you behind - who was she?" Sol asked, glancing down at my hand. I let my fingers slip away - maybe he didn't want me to touch him. The grass smell faded, and I was nose-blind again.

"LuAnn's just someone I met when I was younger. I ran away from a group home and she found me rummaging through the trash for food. She bought me dinner and we talked, and before I knew it, I'd told her all about my weird ability with emotions. She suggested we team up to make a booth to help people and make money."

I knew the explanation was garbled and left out a ton, but my energy was seriously fading. Even though I'd been in a car for hours, I was flat exhausted from all the random shit over the last two days. Not to mention starving, I realized, as the motel door clicked open to show Killian, holding up a plastic gas station sack.

He dumped the food on the table and gestured to us. "I already had mine."

I examined the offerings - a couple of deli sandwiches wrapped in plastic, a bag of cheese puffs, beef jerky, some kind of spicy chips. I raised my eyebrow at him.

"Guy food," I proclaimed, craving something sugary.

"What exactly do you want, kid? A salad? Sparkling water?"

I flushed, not wanting to admit my preferred eating habits, and definitely not wanting to sound like a whiny little kid who needed a sugar fix. "My name is Carlyle, not kid," I grouched instead.

"What a princess," he scoffed. Sol glared at him and made a noise of disapproval around his huge bite of sandwich, but Killian only grinned, pulling a second sack from behind his back.

"Don't worry. I know what Qilin like," he whispered, leaning low. His breath was hot on my ear, and my skin flushed an even deeper pink. Peering into the bag to cover my embarrassment, I bit back a moan.

"*Donuts.*" I tore open the paper bag. He must have found one of those gas stations that had a case of fresh pastries.

"Yeah, that earns me my own bed, for certain," he gloated, his golden eyes flashing at me as I licked white frosting from the top of one pastry. My eyes slid closed as I bit into the fluffy donut and tasted a gooey raspberry filling.

"Wrong goals, man," Sol said, polishing off his sandwich. Killian only shrugged and flopped onto one of the beds, kicking off his boots. He stretched his arms above his head, and I glimpsed the edge of a tattoo on the underside of his bicep, where the short sleeve had ridden up.

I finished the first treat and started a second, loving the shot of energy the sugar gave me. It was way better than caffeine or sleep.

"I always crave sugar right after working with someone's emotions," I told the guys, tipping a bottle of water to my lips.

"Explain this emotion thing," Sol said, ripping open a bag of chips.

"Yeah, we don't know much about your powers," Killian admitted. "As far as we've been trained, Qilin are known for channeling other people's powers, not using their own."

I considered. Maybe what I did with people's emotions could be considered a sort of channeling? If all I could channel was human emotion, though, I had to be the lamest Qilin ever.

I tried to explain the idea of smelling and interpreting emotions, but they both looked at me like I was nuts. Sol was more interested in the fact that my smell-reading power was on the fritz, and the fact that I couldn't push emotions on Jack.

"Try it with me," Sol suggested. "Then we'll know if the Ringmaster has spelled Jack against you somehow."

I nodded, scooting closer to him on the bed. I reached my fingers to his temples, touching lightly, sliding down to the back of his neck, then around to the hollow at the base of this throat, trying to find an easy place to push in. I might as well have been trying to push emotion into a wall - I couldn't feel the tangle of feelings inside him, and I couldn't find any gaps to push mine into.

His breathing slowed and nearly stopped as my fingertips feathered over the muscles in the sides of his neck, across his square, stubbled jaw, and back up to his temples.

I smelled the same cut-grass happiness, mixed with a sharper, richer musk now - something I'd long associated with desire. I drew back quickly, uncertain if I had the right to keep going.

"You didn't feel anything, did you?" I asked, feeling a blush creep up my neck as his liquid brown eyes fastened on mine.

Sol breathed out a sort of embarrassed chuckle. "Oh, I felt something. But I doubt it's what you were going for."

"I was trying to push anger into you," I admitted. I had a surplus of pent-up anger right now, especially when I thought about LuAnn. I really hadn't thought it would work, anyway.

"Nope," he confirmed, scowling at Killian's snicker. "That's not what I got."

He stood and strode for the bathroom, and I bit my lip against a grin when I saw him adjust his jeans around a huge bulge before shutting himself inside. The shower began to run, and Killian burst into laughter.

"Sent him for a cold one, kiddo. Nice work."

I shook my head. "I haven't had problems with my power in years - not since I was first learning to control it. What's different now?" I leaned back in the bed, tilting the water bottle back and forth to see the liquid flow.

"I need a human," I said, a sudden realization popping into my head. "I smelled LuAnn last night, but not Jack or either of you."

"And we're not human." Killian cocked his head, considering. "Maybe your emotion thing only works on non-magical people. Sol," he called. "Little girl and I are going outside for a sec."

Something muffled came back, and Killian snickered. He didn't bother with his boots, only grabbing the key card as he strode from the room. I followed him, leaving the stupid saggy pants. The t-shirt was long enough, and I was pretty much just over it all.

CHAPTER TWELVE

CARLYLE

Killian led the way down the stained concrete steps next to our room and out toward the parking lot. I wasn't sure how far north we'd come, but the night temperature was cooler here, especially on my bare legs. Even though I was tired and sore, it felt good to loosen up and walk a bit, too.

"There were some people smoking out here. Let's just walk by," he suggested.

"The smoke might be hard to work with," I warned.

A group of young guys came into view around a corner, and I felt Killian's hand on my back. He hung back, urging me forward. "You go on. They'll think you're alone at first."

I gathered his plan was to see if the guys would hit on

me, and desire was an easy enough emotion to smell. I slipped into the mindset of working the crowds before a festival night, and I allowed my steps to slow and my hips to sway beneath the loose shirt. I fluffed my hair, pulling it out of its braid - I could do this act in my sleep.

"Hey, gorgeous," one of the guys called, using his heel to grind a cigarette into the concrete.

"Are you looking for a fire extinguisher?" his buddy asked. "Because you're smoking hot."

I swallowed a groan and kept walking. "I heard there was a pool here," I said, close enough now to smell their desire. Yep, my power was definitely working with them. I nearly gagged on the sharp, acetone cockiness they were exuding.

"Nah, no pool. But you can still take that shirt off for me," one said. "You're killing us over here."

I clenched my teeth, trying to keep some kind of a smile on my face. Disgusting pigs - I'd met a thousand like them. Guys like this, who blamed women for their own weaknesses, made me sick.

It was different from the effect I had on Sol, because he hadn't made me responsible or guilty of anything.

"Yeah, no thanks. I'll just head back to my room," I said to the group, starting to turn. One of the guys darted forward and grabbed my arm, and the scents intensified, souring in my belly.

"Look, little girl. You're not any better than us. Just hang out and see where the night takes you."

Anger and pride rolled off of him, swirling in my nostrils like rusted metal and the sizzle of an electric fire. I debated what emotion to push into him, settling on fear. If magic were real, I'd love to fry his balls with a nice little spell.

I sensed the exact moment Killian stepped into view. The rotten fruit scent of unwanted surprise filtered through the other smells, and the guy let go of my arm. I stepped back, bumping straight into Killian. His arm locked around my waist, pressing me flush against his hard body.

As soon as I brought my palm to rest on his forearm, I caught his deep-forest scent - pine needles and green wood. Damn, that was a sexy scent.

"Sorry, babe," he drawled, his voice like a lazy, coiled serpent. "I shoulda walked with you. These guys givin' ya trouble?"

The guys in question backed up, trying to disappear into the shadows.

"No, love," I said, and his arm jerked tighter. "They said there's no pool, so we might as well go to bed."

"Bed sounds wonderful," he said, releasing his arm but twining his fingers with mine. "To bed, then."

I heard one of the smokers mutter something about a lucky bastard as we walked away, and I grinned, barely keeping in my laughter until the motel door shut behind us.

"Did you learn anything?" Killian asked, dropping my hand at once and crossing back to his bed. I frowned at the sudden loss of both contact and camaraderie.

"Yeah, I did," I said, pushing away the odd feeling of hurt. It was better that he wasn't interested in me - I had no business being attracted to either of these guys, much less both of them. "I could smell their emotions, easy. But not yours. That is, until I touched you."

Sol came out of the bathroom just then, and my heart

stopped for a second, then started again in double-time. Holy shit, he was shirtless, and fuck, was it a good look on him. Every smooth plane and golden ridge a girl could want.

"Touched you?" Sol said, eying Killian. He scrubbed a towel over his wet hair.

Killian grinned, not saying a word, and I could tell Sol was getting riled up. I kind of liked the possessive look on his face, though I didn't want to cause trouble between them.

"I touched his arm, and I could sense his emotions. When I let go, they were gone. So humans are easy to read all the time. You guys must be only with touch." I nodded as I thought back to my time on the bridge, and at the kitchen table this morning. I'd been touching Jack, then Sol, each time I'd truly scented their emotions.

"I just can't seem to push anything on you," I added. "How is that helpful?"

"It's not," Killian agreed, ruffling his red hair. "But at least we have more intel."

"Let's get some rest," Sol suggested, settling in the bed next to me. Somehow his massive frame didn't touch my space, but I could feel his body heat warming the sheets. Killian reached up to flick off the lights, and I drifted quickly to sleep, feeling safer than I had in a long time.

When I blinked awake much later, I found myself cuddled right up to Sol's golden heat like a leach. He hadn't moved an inch, and I'd done the opposite of what I'd promised. His face was turned away from me, and his breathing was slow and steady. I battled with my desire to smooth my hands over the planes of his chest and the ripples of his abs.

Suppressing a groan, I peeled myself away as quietly as possible. I slipped into the tiled bathroom and started my shower. It wasn't easy to wash my thick, long hair with the tiny bottles of motel shampoo and conditioner, but getting clean was a must at this point.

Wrapping myself in a scratchy towel, I cracked the door, letting the steam out. It bumped against something, and I found a plastic sack. I sighed in relief when I found a 3-pack of cotton undies, a pair of athletic shorts, a loose green t-shirt, and a new pair of flip-flops. I hurried to get dressed, struggling to finger-comb my wet hair and braid it out of the way.

Killian was on his phone when I came out, typing and scrolling intently. "I'm not much on sizes," he said, without even glancing at me. "But I figured that stuff was hard to screw up. We'll do proper shopping when we get to the new house."

"Thank you," I said, hoping he could tell how much I meant it. "Where's Sol?"

He didn't have to answer, though. Sol opened the motel door just then, balancing a box of donuts and a drink carrier of iced coffees. Starving, I grabbed the box from him.

Then, before I could lose my nerve, I stood on my toes and pressed a kiss on his cheek. He grinned and turned his face quick enough to nip the edge of my lips with his.

It was just cheeky enough to make me want to do a whole lot more.

Feeling my face flush, I stepped back. Opening the donuts, I dove in, sighing around the mounds of icing and creamy filling.

"Jai just sent me coordinates for the new place," Killian

said, picking up a coffee and chugging half of it.

"Hell yeah," Sol said, nodding. "Let's move. You're with me again, shortcake."

"Shortcake?" I asked, raising an eyebrow at him. Were we already at the nickname stage, then?

Sol shrugged. "You smell like cake. And you're short." He shouldered his pack and held the door open for me.

"I am not that short," I snapped as I pushed past, but I was already imagining a huge plate of strawberry shortcake, with ruby-red berries, piles of whipped cream, and-

A low rumble came from Sol, drawing my attention back to him. His eyes were heavy-lidded, and he'd taken on those slinky movements of a predator as he prowled out the door after me. "You shouldn't be making noises like that, shortcake."

"I wasn't making noises!" My stomach growled just as we reached the tiny parking lot, and I glared down at it. Killian snickered and unlocked the car doors.

"You were totally moaning," Sol said as he slid down into the low-slung car. He patted his lap like an invitation, a wicked grin spreading across his face.

"What is this fucking car, anyway?" I griped, scowling at the tiny space left for me. As much as my body was ready for more Sol, I really wished the damn car wasn't a two-seater. A girl could use some space.

Killian glared at me. "This happens ta be a 1964 Ford GT40. Mint. But I donna think that means anything to you."

"Nope," I agreed. "All it means is I have no seat of my own."

"Get your ass in the car, kid," Killian growled. "Qilin or not, I'll leave ya here to bum a ride from those smokers

we met."

I shuddered. That was not an option, even if I didn't really think Killian was serious.

"I don't see how it's still *mint* with the way you drive," I muttered, bending over and sliding my body in on top of Sol's long legs. His arm wrapped my waist and pulled me closer, and I felt his huge erection behind me, pressing right up against my ass. I glanced back at him, eyes wide.

"What?" He was unapologetic this time. "Your *power* is a lot stronger than I expected."

Killian groaned and revved the engine, gulping more coffee before squealing his tires on the way out of the parking lot. I put my concentration into eating two more donuts - without making a sound - and wondering what sort of power I was supposed to have over them.

Jack had said my power was strong too, but he hadn't been very affected by whatever it was.

"I need more info on Qilin," I demanded, licking the last bit of sticky sugar from my fingertips. Now that I wasn't eating, I had no idea where to put my hands.

Sol moved beneath me, and I clenched my thighs together, trying hard to ignore the feel of his cock. It was pretty hard to miss. Killian's brow drew down, and he was shooting daggers down the road. Neither of them said a word.

I set my jaw. "Tell me."

"Shortcake, we just don't know a lot," Sol said. His fingers trailed up my bare arm, and I tensed against a shiver.

"Enough to identify me," I pointed out. "What makes you think I'm one of these creatures?"

"You look like one," Killian muttered. "And you do

have some sort of power over humans."

A couple of minutes ticked by on the dashboard clock as I waited for him to elaborate.

"Wait. That's it?" I snorted. "You do know lots of people look like this, right? Blue eyes and blond hair?"

Killian glanced at me and shook his head. "Your eyes are lavender. Besides, you can't fool my power."

"What power is that?" I filed away the information that he'd studied my eyes closely enough to note their odd color.

"Second sight. I can see through glamor. You're wearing one, and I saw straight through it to your potential shifted form."

I stared at him. "Glamor. Like a disguise?" I'd seen enough TV to know that word, but it didn't make sense. "How am I wearing something I don't know I'm wearing?"

They exchanged a glance over my head. Sol moved again, and I thudded my head back onto his broad shoulder in aggravation. His blond waves tickled my cheek.

"Please tell me someone on your team knows more than you guys do."

"Jai will know," Sol said, his breath warm against my hair as he nestled me deeper in his lap, one arm loose around my hips. His fingers settled on my arm again. After a few minutes of trying to stay tense and keep my hands to myself, I finally relaxed into his warmth, enjoying the tingles racing up and down my body. My hand drifted down to his thigh.

I knew I shouldn't get involved with him - not when I had so little information. Turning my face to the window, I resolved to find out what Jai knew, then make a more informed decision whether to stick with the team or not. I'd always wanted answers, and hopefully this was my lucky break. If not, I was good at disappearing.

CHAPTER THIRTEEN

CARLYLE

"Here we are," Killian murmured as the tires began to crunch gravel.

I rubbed my eyes, pushing back the grogginess I felt from another long day on the road. I wasn't entirely sure where "here" was, but the last signs I'd seen were "Welcome to New York". Rural - not NYC. I hadn't been this far north in a long while.

The car made its way up a steep, winding driveway that seemed to go on way longer than necessary.

"Haven't had this much privacy in years," Killian said as we finally pulled up to a massive stacked-log house. I gaped at its size, wondering if Jai had directed us to a mountain resort instead of a house.

Nestled in among the trees like it had grown there, the building was three sprawling levels with multiple decks wrapping the frame. Woods crept in on all sides, but the top floor was well above the trees, thanks to the slope of the property. An enormous window spanned the height of the house's front, the glass reflecting the trees like a mirror.

"Views for miles," Sol said with a grin, pulling the door handle.

I ducked out of the car, stretching and yawning hard. The air was still summery, but it held the bite of pine needles and felt at least fifteen degrees cooler than where we'd been yesterday. My muscles were crazy cramped - we'd driven pretty much nonstop. I needed a bathroom and food, and I certainly wouldn't say no to a bubble bath.

"With a house this big, Jai must be calling in the whole team," Killian said with excitement, grabbing their backpacks and my plastic sack of clothes from the trunk. He headed up the sloping front walk toward the front door.

Sol glanced back at me. "Finding the last Qilin - that's fucking huge," he murmured. He offered his hand, and I took it, feeling a blush spread over my cheeks.

I was encouraged by the anticipation they both held for seeing their teammates. I still wasn't quite convinced I was the Qilin creature they'd been looking for, but it made me feel a little better about being alone in the woods with virtual strangers.

I mean, bad guys didn't love their team like brothers, did they?

Besides, I had to admit, these two already seemed less like strangers - especially Sol. Something about being near him settled my soul, as if we belonged together like matched pieces of a chess set.

I still needed my independence, sure, but a girl got lonely.

Smiling to myself, I let him lead me to the front door, which was actually two tall wooden doors carved with a vining pattern. Just as we reached the stone steps, the doors both swung in, and I got my first glimpse of the man who had to be Jai. The guys did their fist-bump, man-shoulder thing while I studied the team's leader.

Shorter and slimmer than both Sol and Killian, he wore a pair of low-slung chinos and a black button-up that wasn't buttoned up. It hung open, showing off his sleek, ripped body and a coiled viper tattoo over his left pec. His black hair was pulled straight back from his forehead and smoothed into a tight bun at the base of his neck.

This one was lethal - I sensed it right away. He looked like he knew thirteen ways to slit a man's throat and wouldn't think twice about doing it.

Blocking the doorway, he studied me right back with bottomless black eyes and zero expression on his smooth, chiseled face.

"I'm Carlyle," I said, pulling my hand from Sol's and offering it to shake. I'd kill to touch him and get a whiff of what was going on with his emotions. He glanced down at my hand, then met my eyes again and held my gaze, never blinking. At least it wasn't a challenging gaze - it was searching.

"I must test your blood," he said. The words were so soft that I barely heard them, but as soon as they registered, my heart began to pound. What business did I have giving blood to a *vampire*?

Sol's hand came to rest on my shoulder, the touch light and cautious. "It's okay," he said. "Jai would never hurt you, but he can identify the blood of all the Haretian races. He'll know if you're a Qilin. I can just prick your finger, get one tiny drop, and it'll be done."

"No fangs?" I couldn't help but ask. Killian snickered, but the sound was cut off by a sharp look from Jai.

"Human ideas of vampires have been created and polluted by the worst of my kind. I will not hurt you," Jai said, his expression still blank.

I pursed my lips. I really needed to pee, and it looked like he wasn't going to let me in that gorgeous house without a blood test. I nodded before I could think about it any more.

Sol reached out a hand, and my eyes grew wide again as one of his fingers changed itself into a long, sharp claw. Shit. My sense of reality fuzzed as I reminded myself again these guys weren't human - and most likely, I wasn't either.

Sol smiled tentatively, then lowered his claw to prick the pad of my thumb. I held back any reaction, although I really hated seeing my own blood. A bright ruby bead welled up. I heard Jai breathe deeply, and a low growl vibrated from Sol.

I pushed my hand forward and offered it to Jai, still fully expecting him to lick the blood off me or something.

Instead, he only brushed a forefinger over the drop of blood and sucked his own finger into his mouth. He stared at me, eyes dilating to solid black, then breathed one word. "Qilin."

Before any of us could respond, Jai vanished from the doorstep. He'd moved so fast I hadn't even seen which direction he'd gone.

"You're the real thing, then, kiddo," Killian said, stepping into the house. "Which means I was fuckin' right," he gloated, a cocky grin spreading across his face as he sauntered away.

I rolled my eyes and looked at Sol. "I passed the test, then? What now?"

Sol met my gaze for a long moment, and I saw an unexpected vulnerability in his face. "Now, it's up to you. We do need your help. Remember, though. Qilin always have the right to refuse. You're not bound to us, Carlyle. You can leave this all behind." He blinked away, then he reached for my finger, checking that the blood had stopped.

I let him, because thanks to his touch, I could scent his emotions. There was only truth. It meant a lot that he hadn't played on our attraction or begged me to stay. I still needed a crap ton of answers, but knowing I wasn't trapped here released a ton of tension.

For now, I decided his honesty and respect was enough. Besides, we were in the middle of the woods in upstate New York. Where the hell was I going to go?

"So, can I come into the secret clubhouse now?" I asked. Sol grinned and tugged me inside, squeezing me in a sideways hug as we entered. We moved deeper into the house, checking it out. It was ridiculously massive, rustic and gorgeous. I decided I'd made the right decision in staying.

I excused myself to use the bathroom, then wandered back into the main living room. Stretching my spine over a perfectly-worn leather armchair that could've easily held three of me, I gazed out the picture window into the darkening woods beyond.

"This is amazing," I said to myself.

"Best safe house yet," Killian agreed, ambling past with a thick sandwich already in his hand. He walked all the way to the glass, blocking part of my view. Eh. He added to the view, actually. I found my eyes riveted to the motion of his other arm raising to rest against the glass as he peered down into the strip of yard below, his broad shoulders twisting beneath his thin t-shirt.

"As much as I'd love to pretend I'm on vacation, I'd really like some answers about why I'm here," I called, hoping Jai was in earshot.

"I believe you're here because you're running from a sadistic freak-show master," a low voice said, way too close to my ear.

I stifled a noise that was somewhere between a shriek and a gasp, turning to see Jai standing directly behind my chair. Shit, he was a silent bastard. He moved around the chair and joined Killian at the window, but he leaned his back against the glass and watched me instead of the woods.

"I was told you have those answers," I prodded, righting myself in the chair. Jai turned his face toward Killian and murmured something. I studied his profile - high cheekbones sloping down to a carefully-trimmed line of stubble along his sharp jaw. He was just as gorgeous as the other two, and I couldn't help but wonder at the sheer unlikelihood of these three men looking for me.

"What do you want to know?" Jai asked quietly, making that intense eye contact again. Heat pooled low in my belly, even as a delicious shiver snaked up my spine. He really was beautiful.

"Can you just start from the beginning?" I asked.

Jai nodded, pushing off the window. Sol came in and handed me a plate with a sandwich on it, then relaxed on a deep-cushioned couch. Jai settled on the plush rug before me, looking for all the world like he was about to meditate or bend spoons with his mind or something. "This is Earth."

I snorted, unable to help it. "Maybe not that far back," I said, taking a bite.

His face remained serene. "Earth has a sister planet called Haret. It's populated with all manner of magical creatures. A long time ago, the two worlds were joined by the Path. This Path was always open to those strong enough to survive in both worlds, but the only way to actually travel the Path was via a Qilin."

"So, I'm a magical taxi cab?" I was not impressed with this information.

Jai curled his lip, looking offended. "You are a *goddess*, Carlyle. For a Qilin to accompany - and therefore, bless - a group of travelers was the highest honor. But the innocent generosity of the Qilin was eventually taken advantage of, and the Path was corrupted. First, Qilin began to be kept as part of certain high-powered magical households."

"Like an asset," I inserted, and he nodded. I grimaced. I was not a goddess-for-hire, any more than I was a taxi.

"Then the Qilin began to disappear. Slowly at first, so that by the time the Haret Conclave got around to addressing the problem, Qilin were in danger of extinction. Without the Qilin, the Path itself faded, for their magic actually helps create the Path. Travel between the two worlds has been virtually impossible for many years now. My brothers and I were sent here to find you, and now we are trapped on Earth."

"So you just want me to help carry you home? Then what?" I asked, skeptical of how this actually benefited me. "I'm not sure humanity is ready for a bunch of magicals hopping the border."

"We're not entirely sure what the Conclave plans. Our mission is to simply find you and bring you home."

"Earth is my home," I insisted dumbly. "I was born here."

"Were you?" Jai questioned, and I stared at him. "Do you have proof?"

"Um..." I didn't, actually. I shook my head, my brain sloshing with the movement. "I was found as a baby, in a Buddhist temple. In New York City. The monks contacted Social Services, and I was placed with a string of foster families. So, no. I guess I have no idea where I was born. But if the Path is closed, how would I have gotten here?"

"You're a Qilin," Jai said, his voice patient.

"Ah. So I can cross whenever I want?"

He shrugged. "That is the general belief. We have no way to test it, though."

"Well, where is this Path? Let's try."

He smiled then, and I was rendered breathless. His whole face lit with an inner glow, and he had the most kissable dimple, just on one side. "You've likely seen the Path your whole life. Humans call it a rainbow."

Laughter bubbled out of me, and he frowned. It sounded so ridiculous, though.

"I suppose Killian can help me find the pot o' gold at the bottom, too?"

Killian glared at me, and I felt instantly guilty. "I'm sorry. This is just... a lot." Jai nodded, and I stared down at my half-eaten sandwich, trying hard to take it all in.

I was apparently a Qilin, which was a little like a unicorn - however that worked. And I could supposedly follow a rainbow to another world.

Oh, and I was probably the last of my kind.

No fucking pressure.

CHAPTER FOURTEEN

CARLYLE

I waved the guys away as I stumbled out of a side door in the living room and onto the massive wraparound deck. I just wanted a few moments to process what was passing as reality these days.

As soon as I was alone, I didn't want to be. Somehow, I'd already grown used to Sol and Killian. It didn't make sense, but I missed them. I leaned over the railing, breathing in the smells of the surrounding evergreen forest. It was a pretty refreshing break from emotions, actually. I had so many of my own zooming around in my heart that it was a damn relief not to smell anyone else's.

Several long moments passed, and nothing had really processed. My brain was still a big fucking lump of *nope*. I began to get fidgety and started pacing, muttering to myself.

"Okay, so get over it and pretend all this is true. It would explain why you're so different from everyone. You haven't found any info or met anyone like you because you're the last one."

The part about two worlds wasn't that far gone - I'd never really believed Earth was truly alone in the universe. Hearing that aliens were among us - and had been forever - made so many unexplainable things a lot easier to puzzle out. Believing these aliens were magical also took care of all the random urban legends and cultural myths.

I still wanted some sort of hard-core proof, though. I needed to see some magic - more of what Sol had done with turning his finger into a claw.

The glass door behind me slid open, and I glanced back to see Sol. He didn't say a word, just came to lean against the railing, keeping a friendly distance between us. The early evening was quiet and peaceful, with only a few birds rustling and chirping in the trees beyond. I could sense Sol's body heat, even several inches away.

Suddenly I just really wanted a hug. I wanted to feel his smooth skin more than anything.

"What do you look like? In your shifted form," I asked instead, finally admitting that no amount of staring at some dumbass trees was going to make this any easier.

"I can show you," he offered, cutting his eyes sideways to mine. My heart pounded. I needed this evidence, but if I got it, there was no turning back. Sucking my bottom lip between my teeth, I nodded and stepped back a bit. If my "cracked" memory was even a little bit accurate, he was huge.

"Don't be afraid," he whispered, his deep brown eyes begging the same.

Almost in slow motion, his legs shortened and his palms broadened as they fell to the deck. The wavy gold of his hair grew thick and long, into a luxurious mane, as his face morphed into a muzzle and intelligent feline eyes - *Sol's* eyes, but now as big as my palm. Sun-kissed fur spread down his shoulders, back, and powerful haunches, replacing his clothing and bare skin. And behind him swished a long, sinuous tail.

My hand raised on its own. I wanted to touch him even more now, but I hesitated. My brain was pulsing with the revelation before me. Sol was a shifter. Magic was real. And I couldn't keep hiding from the rippling truths beyond that.

The massive lion before me raised his head and nuzzled my outstretched palm, and I laughed out loud. His rough tongue flicked out and scraped along my palm, tickling it. A rumbly sort of growl vibrated through him, and he lifted a heavy paw to my shoulder. I should have been terrified, but I wasn't.

Instead, I let instinct take over. I rubbed my cheek along the top of his paw, my fingers curling around to the leathery pads beneath. The scent of summer wove around me as I touched the razored tips of his claws carefully, then slowly ran my hand up the muscular leg to his downy underside.

Like a playful house cat, he pulled his paw back and rolled onto his back, batting at the air. I knelt to scratch his belly, grinning hard. I was petting a *lion*. This was so fucking cool.

His paw batted at my back, and I tumbled off balance,

right down into his big lion chest. I felt just a little too much like prey in that position, though. My heart hammered as I scrambled away, scraping my knees on the wooden deck boards.

In an instant, the giant cat before me shifted back to Sol, and his eyes filled with concern.

"It's still me," he whispered, sitting up on the deck and reaching for me with human arms. Somehow his clothes were back, and I let him draw me close against his muscled, fur-less chest. My breathing gradually slowed, and I found myself pressing my cheek against his neck to get even more of his heavenly scent.

That gorgeous swirl of cut grass and hot sun, mixed with his sweet musk of desire radiated over me, warming me from the inside out. I imagined lazy, sun-filled afternoons in bed, surrounded by soft sheets and naked, golden skin. I'd smelled my fair share of desire before, but nothing as deliciously tempting as Sol.

His hand pressed against my hip, nudging me even closer. Everywhere we touched flared with heat. His gentle fingertips brushed along my jaw, tugging my face up.

His lips met mine, slow and careful, seeking permission without a word. I sucked in a breath as the tip of his tongue traced the inside edge of my lips, tasting, just before his teeth closed possessively over the bottom one.

I wanted more than just a taste, and I pushed my fingers through his shoulder-length waves, bringing him closer.

His mouth opened in answer, his tongue stroking mine with a teasing pressure. His hand slipped lower, squeezing my ass as we tried to get even closer. My breasts pressed up between us, and I dropped my head back, encouraging his view.

A predatory growl rumbled in his chest, vibrating my ribcage and all the way to my core. "Yes," I breathed as his lips traced a searing trail straight down my neck and between my breasts, pushing aside my low-cut t-shirt.

I was about seven seconds from telling him to take me to bed or lose me forever, but the sound of the sliding glass door opening behind us popped our little lust-bubble.

I broke free from Sol's grasp and sat back on the deck, trying to catch my breath. Ah, fuck.

It had obviously been way too long, and the desires I'd worked so hard to master were surging back twice as strong.

As he wiped the corner of his mouth and met my eyes with a heated, knowing smirk, I decided I didn't give a flying fuck. I wanted this man, and as long as he wanted me back, I'd make it my mission to taste every inch of that smooth, honey-gold skin. There had to be a dozen beds in this log cabin mansion - we could road-test every last one.

His eyes were like molten chocolate on mine, and I knew he sensed every dirty thought I was having.

Jai stepped silently to where we were still sitting on the wooden boards and stood with arms crossed and feet shoulder-width apart, like a guard. He stared down at us with an unreadable expression.

"I've put out the call. The others should be here within forty-eight hours."

Sol grinned, standing gracefully and offering me a hand up. He did nothing to try and hide his fucking huge erection, either. If anything, he turned his body right toward Jai, and I had to bite back a snort at the alpha male posturing.

Jai lifted the edge of his lip in a silent snarl, baring a glistening white fang. Sol backed down immediately, his shoulders rounding and his eyes going to his toes.

I blinked between them both, surprised at how commanding Jai was without even saying a word. He seriously was the true leader, then. I wondered if he disapproved of Sol kissing me - if it would affect his team. Something told me I didn't want to cross this unassuming vampire.

Then Jai fastened his eyes on me, a glint of interest sparking in their black pools. I really wished I could catch a bit of his scent. Vampires did have emotions, right? I remembered watching a television show with some seriously sexy vampire brothers, and my curiosity spiked. I'd have to find a reason to touch Jai, and fast.

His lips quirked up then in a hint of smile, and I flushed, feeling like a kid who'd been caught with the cookie jar. I swore it was like he had a front row seat to my mental pacing. Before I could phrase the idea into a question, he pivoted on bare feet and slipped back into the house.

"He likes you," Sol said, breaking his submissive pose to throw a casual arm around my waist.

I choked on a laugh. "How can you tell?"

Sol grinned, trailing his fingers down my bare arm. "You're still alive."

"Well, shit. Here I thought I was special or something." I smiled and let Sol press his lips to mine once more. Our tongues tangled together, and Sol backed me against the deck railing.

I spread my palms on the wooden railing for balance as he pressed himself into me, energy and desire zinging throughout my body. I felt like I could sprint for miles, or kiss Sol for days without tiring.

I'd never felt like this with a guy - ever.

Suddenly, a sharp, splintering pain gouged into my palms, chasing away every bit of pleasure. My eyes flew open as I cried out.

"Shit," Sol said, stumbling backward as he stared down at my shaking hands. I blinked at them, trying desperately to understand what had happened. Somehow, the thick wooden railing had shattered beneath my grip, a few splinters shoving their way deep into my palm. My stomach rolled with sickness at the sight of my own blood and the pain coursing through my hand. I looked up at Sol, confusion making my heart race.

"What the fuck?" I whispered, my voice trembling.

Sol only shook his head, a stunned look on his handsome face.

"I don't have that kind of strength," I said. Nothing about this made sense. Had something about being with Sol or the others started to change me? Was I going to shift into a Qilin, now that I knew what I supposedly was? "Where's Jai?" I asked, needing more of the vampire's answers.

Sol scanned the dark tree line, then peered through the window behind us into the house. "I don't know, but we need to get you cleaned up," he said, reaching for my arm. He led me back into the kitchen where he spread out a clean towel and found a first-aid kit, gathering antiseptic cream and tweezers.

I groaned. "Can't someone just magic these splinters out of my skin?" This was going to hurt.

Killian sauntered into the room just then, swearing

when he saw my palms. "How'd that happen?"

I glanced at Sol, but he didn't offer any explanation, so I didn't either. Not that I had one, anyway. I closed my eyes and grimaced as I felt the splinters being tugged from my skin.

"Relax, kiddo," Killian said, moving behind me and beginning to massage my shoulders as Sol worked. I was almost as surprised by his sudden kindness as by what I'd done to the deck railing.

"All finished," said Sol after only a couple of minutes. He rubbed my skin with antiseptic cream, then rose to clean up the mess as I wrapped my palms in a bit of gauze Killian handed me from the kit. Now that the splinters were gone, the pain had gone, too. Killian's hands had also vanished from my shoulders, and I missed the touch more than I wanted to admit.

"I think you should get some sleep," Sol said as he returned. "I'll talk to Jai when I see him, and we'll all figure some things out in the morning."

I didn't like his plan, but I couldn't think of a better one, especially as a huge yawn took over my face. Spent, I followed him up the stairs to my new bedroom, and I crawled under the blankets with heavy eyes.

CHAPTER FIFTEEN

CARLYLE

Even though I'd been sorely tempted to wander into Sol's bed, in the morning I was glad I'd resisted and slept alone.

If I was going to stay with these guys, I needed to be careful not to put out expectations I wasn't ready to uphold. I was used to flings and weekend affairs, not a live-in boyfriend. Slow would work. Maybe.

Pushing back the blanket, I stretched and examined my hands. Oddly, they were completely healed. I hoped Jai would still be up, or that maybe Sol had found out something about my weird strength.

I tested it gingerly on the edge of my bed, finding nothing unusual about my grip now.

The house was silent, and as I crept from room to

room, finding no one, I wondered if I was the only one awake. Every room I peeked into was furnished with simple, rustic decor, soft leather chairs and couches, and deep-pile rugs over polished wooden floors. There were several empty bedrooms and a couple of locked doors.

I eventually began to wonder if I was the only one even in the house, but where would they have gone? And why would they leave me here alone?

My nerves were humming with anxiety by the time I made my way to the kitchen. I couldn't even distract myself by cooking breakfast, because although I found plenty of dishes and pots, there was nothing edible anywhere.

I decided Jai sucked as a safe house setter-upper, and we officially needed to go shopping.

Sugar and coffee were essentials in my life, and even a houseful of gorgeous guys wasn't going to change that.

As I drummed my fingertips on the white marble counter, staring out another wide window into the dense pine trees and debating what to do, the air pressure in the house swelled. My ears ached. I twisted around, but it felt like I was moving in slow motion or pushing through water.

Then the pressure stopped, and my ears popped like when driving through the mountains, up and down over the steep slopes.

I rubbed my jaw, working it to pop my ears a few more times. Footsteps sounded through the front hall, a slow thud-click like solid boots. Fuck, that wasn't good. None of the guys moved like that - Jai was silent, Sol was stealthy but too big for silence, and Killian was always talking.

I grabbed a chef's knife from the block on the counter,

feeling way too much like the dumbass victim in a cheesy horror movie. Hell if I was going to go down without a fight, though.

I darted away from the enclosed counter area toward the dining table. There were doors to the deck here, plus access to the hall.

A tall figure entered the room and stopped abruptly as he spotted me and my big-ass knife.

"Hello," he said, his voice carefully neutral. He eyed my glinting weapon, and I eyed his crazy-expensive black suit. Who wears a suit like that at six in the morning in a log cabin? I immediately didn't trust him. "I'm Alisdair," he began, holding his palms up flat. "You can call me Dair, and I won't hurt you. I'm part of the team."

"Prove it," I demanded, keeping the knife up. I remembered the name, but maybe the guys really weren't sleeping peacefully. Maybe something had happened to them. This man could be the Ringmaster himself, for all I knew. I'd never actually seen the man. Add a top hat, and he'd about have the costume down.

"How exactly would you suggest I do that?" he asked, a hint of a smile on his beautiful face. Damn, I hoped he wasn't a bad guy, because he was seriously hot. His clothes and the tight set of his shoulders made him seem older, but I could tell by his thick-lashed, dark blue eyes and smooth, creamy skin that he wasn't much more than early twenties.

"That's your burden," I said, stalling for time. I had no idea, really, how he could prove my request without one of the guys showing up.

"How else would I know the location of Jai's new safe house?" he tried. I raised an eyebrow, rejecting the question. For the right people, it shouldn't have been hard to track our movements. Jack had found me once, and he could find me again.

We continued our state-off, which unfortunately only gave me more time to fixate on his good looks. He was built strong but slim, and tall, nearly to the doorframe he'd stopped in. Black hair, left just long enough that I could see a generous, fat curl to it, but pushed away from his open face. Full, Cupid's bow lips that were now twisting into a grin beneath the hint of black stubble.

"Never mind. Our problem is solved," he said, but before I could question him, the front door banged open. I heard Killian's boisterous laugh, accompanied by Sol's deep rumble, and soon the two of them were shoving Dair away as they barged into the kitchen.

Sol unloaded about eight grocery bags, and Killian plonked a large cooler on the floor.

"Dair," Killian nodded. Sol gave him a sort of bro hug, bumping shoulders and knuckles at the same time.

Dair flicked his long fingers at me, and the knife slipped right from my grasp. I gasped as it flew across the kitchen and inserted itself neatly into the wooden block.

"Asshole," I muttered, feeling my skin flush at the realization that I'd not only given him a hard time for no reason, but that he could have bested me at any second. Instantly, his tall form was across the room and crowding me into the back windows. The back of my bare legs pressed against the cool glass, and I wished was wearing something more than an oversized t-shirt.

"Damn straight, I'm the asshole," he said, his low voice like ebony silk across my ear as he leaned down. None of his body touched mine, but fuck if I didn't feel his words slide all over me in the most sensual way. "And none of my women would have had it any other way."

"I'm not your woman," I said, glaring up at him, although my body was already raising its flag in surrender. My nipples were poking up through the thin fabric of my shirt like they were yelling, "Take me!"

"We'll see about that," he said, his words barely a breath as he turned away and walked out of the room, his polished black boots making that unhurried thud-click noise again, the sound resonating deep in my belly with every measured step.

I took in a deep, shaky breath and looked back to Killian and Sol. Sol had his head stuck in the fridge, stocking the groceries, but Killian caught my eye. I balked at the anger in his stare, but he hid it quickly.

Why would he be *mad* at me? Because I'd threatened Dair? Or was it because I'd just kissed Sol last night, but I'd obviously been affected by Dair's words?

Damn. I definitely did not want to break their guy code, or team dynamics, or whatever.

He shoved a hand through his messy red hair, standing it up, and muttered something under his breath. He opened the cooler and replaced Sol, stacking pizzas in the freezer compartment.

"Where's Jai?" I asked, since he still hadn't appeared.

"Probably sleeping," Sol said with a shrug, shoving boxes of cereal into a cupboard. "He's more of a night owl."

"Oh. Vampire, right. So, sunlight burns him?"

Both guys laughed. "Not exactly," Sol answered. "He doesn't suck blood from virgins, either, but I'll let him explain his abilities and weaknesses when he's up."

108

"Really?" I huffed, hands propped on my hips. "Again with the secrets? I'm staking my life here, and all you want to do is tell me shit later. Well, it's later. So spill."

Killian chuckled and gestured to Sol as if to tell him to have at it. I huffed and began rummaging in the remaining bags, looking for something that didn't have to be cooked. I was starving and getting downright grumpy with the whole crew.

CHAPTER SIXTEEN

CARLYLE

Before I could find anything immediately edible, Dair opened the door behind me, somehow coming in from the deck this time. I scooted out of his way, not ready to feel his dark gaze on me again.

I couldn't help but wonder what he smelled like. Of course, I'd have to touch him. Which wouldn't be bad, either. I shook my head, jumping off that speeding train of thought.

"Perimeter is reinforced now," Dair said.

I leaned against the ginormous wooden dining table, debating asking him what that meant. I wasn't as comfortable pushing him as I was with Sol. Something told me he would push right back. Hoping to distract myself until Sol had finished making coffee, I stared around the room. I counted seven chairs around the table - three on each side and one at the head. I glared at it, imagining Dair was the type to claim head of table.

"Hungry?" Sol asked, coming around the kitchen island with a hand behind his back. I nodded, feeling almost frantic, and he brought his hand around, presenting me with a perfect, pink cupcake. I squealed and grabbed for it, but he drew it back, swiping his finger through the frosting. He smiled and lifted it to his mouth, and hungry rage clicked over my eyes. I yanked his hand down and sucked his finger into my mouth, claiming all the sugary goodness for myself.

"Fuck," he whispered, his eyes round as saucers. I heard one of the others choke behind us, but my eyes were locked on Sol's.

"Mine," I said around his finger, grabbing the cupcake and releasing him. I plopped down into the head chair, staring around the room like an animal guarding its kill.

"Fuck yeah, it's yours, kiddo," Killian said, although there was an edge of mocking to his voice. I felt another urge to address his stupid nickname for me, but the rich smell of the cupcake won out, and I unwrapped it, licking every bit of frosting from its paper. Biting deep into the cake, I slumped back into the large chair, eyes sliding closed.

"Perfection," I murmured around another huge bite.

"So that story is true, anyway," Dair said, his velvety voice an obvious contrast to Sol's rumbles and Killian's bite. I slitted my eyes open when something clunked on the table before me.

Coffee. I hummed in pleasure at the steaming mug as

Dair slid into the seat at my right hand. I heard Sol grumble a bit, and soon he was shoving himself into the chair at my left. The two men faced off, staring each other down in some sort of whose-is-bigger contest. I took another bite of cake, content to watch the show. Hell, maybe they'd whip it out for comparison, and I'd really win big.

Like he'd read my mind, Killian scoffed. "Boys, we all know my dick is the biggest. And neither of you remembered the sugar to sweeten the girl." He stood behind my chair and reached around to set the sugar bowl next to my mug. "You have to know how to tame the beast," he snickered in my ear, and I twisted in my chair to glare at him.

"Fuck off," I said. "I am not a beast, and while we're on it, I'm not a goddamn kid, either."

"You're not a lot o' things," he snorted, his face heating with anger as he backed away. I blinked, trying to make sense of his words, but he only stalked out of the room.

"More for us," Dair said, splaying his palms wide on the table. Sol rumbled something that sounded like "fuck you," but I ignored both of them as I spooned sugar into my coffee.

I downed half the dark sweetness before glancing back to Dair. "What story?"

He examined me for a long moment, and I bristled. If he was going to start this secret-keeping shit, too, I was out of here.

Then he smiled, and I nearly forgot my own name. Holy shit, he needed to do that more often. Or never again, maybe. His lips parted even more as I tried to tear my gaze from his. I pressed my mug to my face, drinking deeply. It was the only thing saving me from lunging across the table and crawling into his lap.

Goddamn hot men and their goddamn smiles.

"There are a lot of old stories and rumors about Qilin. I know they can't all be true, but it appears the cravings for sugar are a very real thing," he answered.

"Lots of people love sugar," I said, eying the bakery box on the counter. I wanted another cupcake, but I felt embarrassed getting one, now that we were analyzing my eating habits. Luckily, I didn't have to decide, as Sol scraped his chair back and fetched the whole box for me. There were five more luscious treats in the box, each in a different shade of pink. I sighed in bliss as I chose another and swirled my tongue around the piped frosting.

"I don't think I've met someone who loved sugar quite the way you love sugar," Dair said, his tone teasing. "It looks like you're mouth-fucking that cupcake."

I choked on said cupcake, feeling my cheeks heat. Dammit, now I really felt weird about eating it.

"Don't ever stop being what you are," Sol said, his voice much quieter than normal, his eyes dropping to his clenched fists. The words tugged at my heart a little, and I wondered if he'd felt the pressure to resist his lion side.

Being a shifter had to be a lot harder to hide here on Earth. If I truly was one of these Qilin creatures, that meant I'd have a different form, too.

I reached over and squeezed one of his fists between my palms. Once our skin was touching, his scent bloomed around me, and I breathed in the summer aroma, noting how this time, it was cut through with a bite of chemical regret and singed-hair disgust.

"You're ashamed? Why?" I whispered, interpreting the scents.

I pressed my fingers into his skin, tugging at the negativity. It still resisted my power to push and pull, but at least now I could sense it.

Sol didn't answer. He broke our touch, standing abruptly and stalking out of the room. I blinked and pressed down my frustration. We were still practically strangers. It was one thing to demand answers about myself but entirely different to pry into his past.

Dair leaned back in his chair, one palm resting casually on the table, fingers tapping in a slow back-and-forth pattern. His suit jacket was unbuttoned, and I studied the textured vest beneath.

He was dressed for Wall Street, and I was in a shapeless t-shirt and plain cotton underwear. I picked at my cupcake, my appetite not very strong anymore.

"So where's the last guy?" I asked. I'd met Killian, Sol, and Jai. Now Dair. Jack was hopefully not invited. That left the sixth man unaccounted for.

"I'm supposed to tell Jai first," Dair began, but I cut him off with a huff. Shoving my chair back, I stood and dumped my half-eaten food in the trash. I was so done with the secrets.

I filled a glass of water from the tap to clear the sweetness from my mouth, suddenly not wanting any of these stories to be true. As I stood in front of the sink, staring out the window into the misty tree line, I heard Dair's boots come to rest just behind me. His body covered mine and slowly pressed into me from behind, lean and rock hard. He bent his head down to my ear and inhaled, and we were so close I could feel every inch of his cock hardening between us, pressing into my ass.

I knew I should stop him - and somehow I knew he *would* stop, but instead I was white-knuckling the counter just to keep from reaching back to grab his body.

"Toro is compromised, like Jack. He's not with the Circus, but he's gone rogue."

Those simple words - the act of sharing his valuable information - heated me straight through, and I felt my core clench with need. Again.

I gritted my teeth. What I needed was to get a motherfucking grip. I'd ogled Killian and Jai, then I'd kissed Sol last night. I couldn't very well turn around and make a move on Dair, no matter how much I wanted to.

"Jai told me you don't know much about yourself," he murmured against my ear. "None of us really have that problem, and I apologize that my brothers have made this difficult for you. But Carlyle, you could be like a savior to us and our world. A goddess. We can't afford to compromise the natural development of your power with faulty information based on rumor. We need you to discover your magic as the natural laws of Haret intended."

I opened my mouth to demand an explanation, but the words died in my throat as his fingers slid down my bare arms. Every bit of skin he touched flamed to life, and I breathed in the truth of his words.

Dair's scent was as dark and gorgeous as he was, all sweet tobacco and sparkling, crystal goblets of dry champagne. His fingers slipped between mine, loosening my grip on the counter, and I rested my head back on his chest. His hips pressed mine even harder into the edge of the counter, pinning me just at the edge of pain, and heat flared between my legs.

A soft moan slipped from my lips as he drew our joined hands over my hips, dipping in at my waist, then bumping up over my ribs. I was feeling my body through his fingers, and it was intoxicating. I was about to whisper that he wasn't an asshole after all when his fingers pulled mine over my breasts and pinched my nipples so hard I cried out at the unexpected touch.

Dair untangled our fingers, then pressed my palms over the tight, tender buds, encouraging me to massage the pain away. One of his hands gripped the side of my throat while the other cupped hard between my legs, nearly lifting me off the floor. He yanked my head to the side and crashed his lips onto the exposed, sensitive skin of my neck. He sucked almost violently, and an arrow of sweet pain shot straight down to where his fingers clenched around my sex.

I was thrumming with energy again, but my body was confused by his mastery of sweet and sharp. One of my hands pressed harder into my breast, chafing and pinching at my nipple again, while the other scratched at his grip on me. His fingers curled, pressing the fabric of my underwear tight against my aching pussy, and I bucked against him, wishing there was nothing between us. Dair chuckled, the sound sultry and commanding all at once.

"Naughty *and* demanding, aren't you. I'll give you everything you want, but we have to build up to that sort of trust, Carlyle. Cariño," he murmured, releasing me and stepping back in one fluid motion.

The sudden loss of heat and touch made me groan, and I turned and reached for him, only to have him vanish into thin air with the same sort of ear-popping that had begun my odd morning.

Alone in the kitchen, I slumped against the counter and tried to gather my wits. My hair was a tangled mess, the neck of my t-shirt was stretched out so far it hung around my shoulder, and my undies were soaked. All of this from maybe two minutes with Dair? Barely twelve hours since I'd kissed Sol and destroyed the deck railing?

Yep, I was fucked.

CHAPTER SEVENTEEN

CARLYLE

Since all the guys had vanished, and I'd lost my appetite, I padded back upstairs to check out my bathroom.

It was a treat to have all this space to myself - more peace and quiet than I'd ever had. Maybe even too much, I decided as I explored.

I'd been hoping for a tub to soak in, but instead there was a hell of a fancy shower. Jets came at me on three sides, and I fiddled with the handles, groaning when I found the massage setting. Someone had stocked the shower with lots of yummy-smelling products, so I took my sweet time.

When I returned to my bedroom, squeezing my wet hair with a towel, two crisp department store bags waited on the bed. I glanced around, but there was no evidence of who had left them. Maybe I should start wrapping a towel around myself if they were just going to barge in my room whenever they wanted.

Peeking in one bag, I saw a pair of super-soft leather ankle boots with enough substance to run or kick the shit out of someone, but enough buckles to look cute. Beside them were a pair of black sneakers and an assortment of socks. Dumping over the second bag, I held up a pair of dark, velvet-soft skinny jeans, then some high-quality black leggings with a leather strip up the side. Next, I found several silky, knit tops in black, camel, and gray. There were even a couple of sexy but comfy-looking workout outfits.

I'd thought the bag was empty, but at the very bottom, wrapped in tissue paper, were several pairs of skimpy, gorgeous panties with matching lacy bras, all in dark colors.

I sighed, running my fingers over the expensive fabrics. There were no price tags or receipts, but I could tell just by the feel of the fabrics that this gift cost more than any clothes I'd ever owned. Probably more than all the clothes I'd ever owned.

I slid into a pair of plum-colored lace underwear and one of the front-clasp bras, then the leggings and a light gray top. The neckline cut low, the style slipping off my shoulder just a bit to show the delicate lace strap of my bra. The hem was gathered in to fit my waist, and the sleeves were long, just past my wrists.

Hell, it fit me like it had been sewn on my body, and the fabric was so soft and light it was as good as being naked in a warm room. Part of me didn't want to accept the clothes - I'd owe someone big time. As I checked myself out in the mirror, skimming my hands down the edgy look, I gave up on that idea.

I was comfy, *and* I looked badass.

Whoever had left this bag deserved a special kind of thanks. Given the color selection and the high quality, I had a pretty good idea who to thank. My belly flipped at the thought of Dair's dark, sleek suits, imagining how that slick fabric would feel against my skin.

I tried on each outfit, falling more in love with the new look by the second. Changing back into the leggings, I luxuriated in having the time to fully dry my hair into the soft waves I loved best.

Feeling like a whole new person, I practically skipped downstairs. The aroma of tomato sauce and fresh bread drew me straight to the kitchen, and I was shocked to realize it was nearly lunchtime. My steps slowed as I reached the closed door, suddenly hesitant to see anyone. Several male voices reached me, though the words were muffled.

I wasn't sure how I fit in their group yet. Killian thought of me as a little kid, while Sol and Dair seemed ready to fight over me. Jai was a complete mystery, topped only by the unknown fates of Jack and Toro.

I knew if I was going to be part of this group, I wanted to be helpful. Not a burden. Not a plaything.

All my life, I'd dreamed of having a family. Doubt shadowed my thoughts, but even more now, I wanted to believe that joining the guys in the next room could turn into something I'd assumed I'd never have.

Taking a deep breath, I pushed open the kitchen door. They were all gathered - even Jai, who surprisingly, was the one stirring the sauce. He brought a spoonful of sauce to his lips and tasted it, his eyes locked on me.

I blinked away from his intensity, turning to Sol instead. He smiled at me, though his eyes narrowed as his gaze wandered over the clothes. Killian barely glanced up, intent on his phone, but Dair stood and pulled out the head chair like a damn gentleman in the movies, gesturing for me to sit.

"Thanks for the clothes," I said, my voice low enough to only reach Dair. I kept my eyes straight forward on the back window, feeling my cheeks heat. I could see his smirk from the corner of my eyes, and when I dared a glance, my skin flushed even more beneath his heated stare.

"Of course," he murmured, leaning over me and taking my empty plate. My body heat spiked at his nearness, though he hadn't even touched me. He crossed to the stove top and dished out noodles and sauce. The others lined up to fill their plates, but Dair served me first. The plate clinked before me, then he set his own down and handed me the basket of bread.

My fingers brushed his, and something like electricity sparked across my knuckles. I nearly dropped the bread, but Dair's face was as smooth as granite. Had he even felt that?

Everyone returned to the table, and I dug in, groaning around the first bite. Hell yes, the vampire could cook. The sauce was wonderfully full of flavor, and the bread had a perfect crust to it. I could definitely get used to treatment like this.

"So what's the plan? The next step?" I asked, running my eyes over the four of them as we ate.

"Yeah, Boss, what is the next step?" Sol turned to Jai.

Jai pursed his lips. "I think our previous strategy of splitting up is done. We've lost track of two team members this cycle. Now that we have found Carlyle," he nodded to me, "the first portion of the mission is complete. We just need to locate and extract Toro and Jack before we can move to the second portion."

"What's that?" I asked, since the others murmured agreement.

"Finding a way home to Haret," Killian said, gazing out the back window into the overcast sky.

That's right. I was their ticket home. But... "What do you mean, finding? Don't you know how to get home?"

"It's not that simple, love," Dair said, wiping a speck of sauce from his full lips with a napkin. "It isn't like showing a passport or driving across a border. Haret is effectively in another dimension. We have to *find* the Path before we can follow it."

"I see rainbows all the time," I protested. If they were the Path, I was missing some piece of the puzzle.

"Have you ever tried to find the bottom of one?" Killian pointed out. "Impossible. The Path is out there, but finding the actual place to hop on is a bit more challenging."

"Wouldn't it just be in the same place where you came here?" I continued, still not seeing their problem.

"I see," Dair said, glaring around the table.

"See what?" I demanded, anxiety tightening my chest. What had they been keeping secret?

"None of them has had the balls to tell you the full truth. You see, Cariño, the longer we stay on Earth, the more we forget about home. And we've been here a very, very long time."

"How long?" I was afraid to know his answer.

"Nearly a hundred years," Sol said, his voice so low I barely caught it. I choked on a bite of bread and grabbed my glass of water, hoping to wash down the feeling of betrayal, too.

I mean, a hundred years? Not only had I made out with two guys in two days, but both of them were a hundred fucking years old. Older! Because obviously they hadn't been dumped on Earth as babies.

"How old *are* you?" I glared daggers around the table.

CHAPTER EIGHTEEN

CARLYLE

They all looked to Jai, the damn cowards. He sighed, but he met my eyes and accepted my fury with a nod.

"Haretians… well, we don't age while on Earth. Our bodies thrive here, though our minds eventually fail. We must return to Haret to cleanse our minds, but then our bodies age. So, we aren't immortal, but our strange stasis has likely given rise to many humans' stories of immortality," Jai explained.

This didn't exactly answer my question, and it brought up a whole flood of new ones. "But I'm from Haret, right? Why am I aging?"

Dair said, "Most likely, your body hasn't finished growing. Both humans and Haretians typically grow in height until around your age."

I considered this. At nearly twenty-one, it was hard to tell if I was aging physically or not. It was a little early for wrinkles. I hadn't gotten any taller in a year or two, but my body had filled out more in the past few years, from sticks and twigs to hips and breasts.

"So how old are you in Haretian years? Is it kind of the same?" I needed a number.

"Kind of," Sol answered, nodding, and I huffed out a breath of relief. "Counting like a human would, I'm twenty-one, Kills and Toro are twenty-two, and Dair and Jai are twenty-four. Jack's the baby at barely twenty."

That made me feel marginally better - I was somewhere between Jack and Sol. Still, the amount of experience these guys had with the world? It was mind-numbing. They'd lived here on Earth through so much change.

"Wait. So you've been looking for *me* for a hundred years?" Maybe they weren't so bright after all. I mean, they'd been a little early to the party.

Killian snickered and rolled his eyes. "We've been looking for any Qilin. Your mother would have worked, too. Or your father, but obviously, we weren't sent to mate with him."

"Ew. So you were going to mate with my mother to save the world, but I'll do in a pinch?" That was gross. I'd never even met my mother, but I didn't like feeling like I was interchangeable with her.

"*Bonding* is highly personal," Jai corrected. "None of us - or you, for that matter - is expected to mate and create a life-bond. It is in no way part of our mission." He glared around the table at each guy like he was giving orders, and I was amused to see Sol and even Dair lower their eyes to their leader.

I nodded, feeling a little better that I wasn't, like, suddenly betrothed to a bunch of mega-hot strangers. Kissing and a little playing around was one thing, but mating made me think of animals, and bonding sounded too much like forever.

Forever made my independence itch.

Jai continued, "There were dozens of teams sent when the Path was on the verge of collapse. The plan was to find as many missing Qilin as possible, bring them to our headquarters on Earth, and work on rebuilding the Path from this end."

"Was?" I noticed his use of past tense for the plan.

Jai's lips pressed together, and his eyes narrowed in fury. I caught the assassin vibe again, and I shrank back against my seat.

"Our headquarters on Earth have been severely compromised in the last decade. We can no longer rely on them for updated intel or safety in crisis. All progress on the Path has been lost. Many of the teams have disappeared or gone rogue, and too many others are confirmed dead. Someone is hunting Haretians here on Earth, and if we don't restore the Path, Haret is doomed as well. Our world cannot function as a closed environment - without a connection to Earth and the imagination, curiosity, and innate innocence of humans, our magic grows darker every day. Without even a single Qilin to restore the Path, Haret will be consumed with its own darkness, like the collapse of a dark star."

"Wow," I whispered. If things hadn't sounded serious before, they sure as shit did now. "Fuck. This is nuts."

Sol reached across the table and squeezed my hand.

"I'm sorry so much of this falls on you, shortcake. We'd all do it ourselves if we could."

I chewed on my bottom lip and nodded. I believed him - I could scent the honesty as well as see it in his eyes. I hadn't known any of them long, but I trusted them. They'd kept me safe from the Ringmaster when they didn't have to, and they'd fought one of their own to do so.

They'd treated me well - like I mattered. Like I was desirable, in Sol's case, and Dair's.

I took a deep breath and flicked my eyes around the table. "Thank you. All of you. Whatever comes next, I really want to help."

Each of them nodded or murmured thanks, and I smiled. I could do this. I could learn to be a real, helpful member of their team. Now that I'd seen how they cared for each other, I was even more hopeful that I'd find the sense of family I yearned for.

Jai leaned back in his chair, his food finished. "I believe the next steps must be to locate and retrieve Jack and Toro. I won't leave a man behind, and we need our full team strong. We've evaded the mystery hunters this long - we can do it while we track down the dragon and the sea prince."

"I was working on a lead for Toro before you called me in," Dair said. "I can continue that from here for a few days, but a lot of it was on-the-ground work."

Jai nodded. "Three days, then we'll reevaluate."

"Jack is with Underbelly," I said, my brain scheming. "And they want me. So while we're looking for Jack, the Ringmaster will be searching for me."

"Nope. Uh-uh. Don't even think about being bait," Sol snapped. I glared at him, annoyed because he'd guessed my unspoken plan so easily.

"He was an asshole to me, but if all that was because of some spell the Ringmaster put on him, then I want to help him," I said, not even remotely interested in giving up my idea.

"If he was an asshole, it was definitely Underbelly," Killian agreed. "Jack's a softie."

Sol chuckled. "We give him a lot of shit for it, too. The mighty dragon who's more like a baby lizard."

"He seemed pretty powerful to me." I grimaced, remembering the flaming fireball he'd sent at our previous safe house, and the way he'd viciously fought Sol and Killian in the parking lot.

"It means a lot that you want to help him," Jai said, his soft voice breaking into our discussion.

Dair smiled. "It's a sign."

"A sign?" I repeated. "Of what? I've always liked helping people."

"Qilin are like that," Dair reminded me. "But it takes a lot to want to help someone who hasn't been kind - someone who's threatened you, even. It shows your natural instincts."

I considered, still not sold on the idea. Knowing a name for what I was - what they thought I was - helped some. Unfortunately, it hadn't helped fill the hole in my identity very much. A name didn't make me feel different or give me more power.

"I need some more training," I blurted. "Like how to fight and use a gun or whatever, and magic stuff." Crap, this time I really did sound like a lame little kid. "I've escaped the Ringmaster's people twice now, but Jack was the strongest one yet. I couldn't have beat him on my own."

"Hold on," Sol said. He glanced around at the other guys, and they all shook their heads. "We didn't realize you'd already had a run-in with the Circus."

I shrugged. "I've known about the Ringmaster for a long time. I met some girl at a festival, and she tried to get me to come meet her friend, who I found out later was one of the Ringmaster's recruiters. I don't think they knew what I was, though. They didn't push me to join them, only suggested that Underbelly was a good place for runaways to find a family. It was tempting, but something didn't seem right. A couple of years later, I came across the same girl, and this time, she'd been looking for me. She didn't give up very easily that time." I shuddered, remembering the fight I'd had trying to get away.

"You fought her off?" asked Killian, one eyebrow cocked in disbelief.

I scowled. "I haven't exactly had the luxury of training, but I got a few lucky hits in. I managed to slice her cheek with my blade and run. I'm decent with a knife." I knew I sounded defensive, but life had been crap to me. I'd learned what I could from the few people who cared, but some real lessons would go a long way.

I glanced around the table, relieved to find at least Sol looked impressed. "After that, I started being really aware of where I was. I started listening harder, and I started asking subtle questions of people I met on the road. I found out the Ringmaster has several circus camps around the country, and he might even have some outside of the United States. Nobody seemed to know where the main camp was, but if he has Jack, I bet he's there. He seems like a really valuable person."

"He's valuable to the Ringmaster, I'm sure, but he's more valuable to us as our teammate," Jai said, his words soft.

"He's more than a teammate. He's our goddamn brother, and we're getting him back," Killian said, his eyes hard.

I felt the shift in the air as determination rippled around the table. Suddenly, these guys were a million times more intimidating. I shivered a bit, realizing I was eating pasta with a table full of killers. Good guys or not, these men were prepared to do whatever it took to find Jack and Toro.

CHAPTER NINETEEN

CARLYLE

The kitchen was too quiet, and I was growing restless while all the guys stewed over their manly revenge plots. Gathering my silverware, I started to get up.

Sol reached out a hand to stop me. "What happened to you, Carlyle?" he asked, his voice low and soothing. His hand pressed over mine. "How did you come to be so alone, and know literally nothing of who you are?"

The others turned to hear my answer, and I rubbed my shoulder with the opposite hand, recognizing my stress cramps beginning.

The story needed to be told, but there was nothing that could make it easier to tell. Unless it was the fact that my story was starting a brand new chapter, and being alone was hopefully not part of it. I took a calming breath, staring at the wood grain of the table and focusing on the warmth of Sol's touch.

"I don't know anything about my parents. I was found in a New York City Buddhist temple, all alone and wrapped up in a dirty blanket. The only thing with me was a note with my name. The monks at the temple took care of me for a few days. They couldn't find a permanent home for me, so I ended up in Social Services. That was okay for a few years. Really young children are easy to place with great families. As I got older, though, it got a little harder."

I was silent for a few seconds as I thought about some of the odd and ugly things that had happened to me. In the context of all I'd learned about myself, so much of my past made sense now.

"Obviously, nobody knew what to make of my weird ability to tell what people are feeling. A lot of the foster families were creeped out, with a few of them even feeling like I could read their minds. It got worse when I was about thirteen. One of my foster brothers had a crush on me, and my power was all over the place. I didn't like him, but every time he'd touch me, I'd feel this crazy rush of desire. It was so confusing - to both of us. I couldn't understand why my body seemed to want him when my brain didn't. He started to call me a tease."

There were a couple of sharp intakes of breath from the guys around the table as they processed what I was saying.

"Shit," Sol breathed. "You were taking his emotion and passing it back to him, like a circle."

I nodded, slumping in my chair. "It was like a fire that just kept growing. It's hard to claim assault when your own fucking body keeps reaching for the enemy." I bit my lip, hating the bitterness I'd let slip out. I was working hard to shut down each emotion like I'd taught myself over the years, locking it away in a dark corner of my brain.

Still, I couldn't shake the nausea that bubbled up at the memory of his clammy hands on my body.

The more my foster brother had touched, the more my body responded. My power must have soaked in his emotion and pushed it back twice as strong - he would have been drowning in teenage lust.

It made sense now, but I was shaking as I forced away the guilt and the confusion I'd struggled against for so many years.

"I hated my body - it was a goddamn traitor to what my heart wanted," I whispered.

"Carlyle, I…" Sol began, his face wrought with guilt. He started to withdraw his fingers from mine.

"No," I said, sitting forward and grasping his hand harder. His touch was one I *did* want. I glanced at Dair to let him know I was thinking of him, too. "I'm in control now. Not my power."

I was reassuring myself as much as him. I had been feeling very out of control around Sol, and now Dair, but it was a heady, breathless rush. Definitely not the same sluggish, desperate scrabbling I'd felt at thirteen.

"Anyway. When I complained to my caseworker, I got a lot of backlash from the family, claiming I was trying to ruin their son's life. We were both underage, and it looked pretty consensual from the outside. The caseworker tried to place me in another home, but my record was shot.

Unfortunately, the only place left at that point was a group home."

I fiddled with my fork, really not wanting to continue. I didn't want to be dramatic. I knew a lot of people had worse stories, and that my story could have been a hell of a lot worse. None of that made it any easier to say out loud, though.

Finally, I said, "The group home was a lot harder."

"It's okay, Cariño," Dair whispered. "It's all in the past."

"What's *Cariño*?" I asked, stalling. I glanced to Jai, who was white-knuckling the table, his black eyes fixed on me. He hadn't made a noise, but I felt the rage rippling from him. Killian was staring out the window into the trees, his sharp jaw clenched.

"It means 'my sweet,'" Dair replied simply, slipping a hand onto my thigh under the table. The touch was more soothing than sexy, and it fortified me enough to rush through the rest of the story. Now that I'd started, I really wanted them to know it all.

Sol stroked his thumb across my palm, and I began again.

"Once I got to the group home, I had a whole new set of problems. A couple of the girls were jealous of me for some reason. The older guys who passed through were always trying to hit on me or corner me and shit. I learned how to hide and avoid, but it didn't always work. My fucking power was so hard to control. Rumors spread that I was a slut."

I huffed out a deep breath. I hated that goddamn word.

"One of the girls finally got on my side when I helped her through some other things, and she was the one who taught me a little self-defense. I stole a knife and practiced every second I could. I was also learning more control over the emotion thing, though I still didn't understand it. At least I could tell what were my emotions and what weren't, which helped with the guilt I felt every time a boy cornered me for sex or whatever. If I fought back, they said I was playing *slut games*, and they'd get rough. For a while, it was safer to just let it happen."

I ignored Killian's curse and the growl coming from Sol. Now I just wanted to finish - this was the worst part.

"Eventually, I figured out that I could choose which emotions to push back on people, rather than just reflect them like a mirror. I just wasn't very good at it, and a lot of times I ended up pushing fear or anger on them instead. One night, there was this particular boy who struggled with self-harm and chronic depression. I freaked out when he found me in my bed. I pushed my fear on him, and it must have tipped him over the edge of reason. He... he killed himself right there in my room, with a gun I hadn't even known he had." I swallowed hard, shoving down the panic that still battered my chest, even after all these years.

I'd woken to the sound of that gunshot for hundreds of nights afterward, my mind pulsing with the horror of seeing someone put a gun to their temple and pull the trigger. Even now, I could feel the hot weight of his body as it fell on me, and a trickle of sweat slid down my spine as I scrubbed my face, like I was still cleaning off the gore.

"Carlyle," Jai said, his voice low but just sharp enough to hook me back to reality. I nodded, forcing my breathing to slow.

"I was absolutely terrified. I *made* him do that," I said, choking on the admission. They needed to know what I was capable of. "It was the same with Jack - I tried so hard, but I still couldn't help him." I hung my head, my hair like a pale curtain separating me from them. I wondered how this story would change their feelings for me.

Killian slammed his fist on the table, and I cringed, glancing at him in surprise. "Donna ever think any o' tha' was your fault, Carlyle," he said, his voice firm as he glared at me. His eyes flashed gold, and I nodded automatically, my eyes wide. He was the last one I'd expected forgiveness from.

Jai murmured his agreement, just as Dair squeezed my leg. Sol tightened his grip on my fingers. I fought for a smile, managing a weak one.

These guys didn't blame me for their brother, and the other boy was an unchangeable part of my past. As I locked away the final memories, I vowed to try and give myself the same break.

I sat up straighter and raked my hair back, ready to finish my story.

"I was panicked that somebody would figure out a way to blame me and press charges, and I'd end up in a cell somewhere. So, I grabbed what I could and climbed out the window. Once I was out on the street, things got a little better in some ways, but a lot worse in other ways. It's not easy for a skinny kid to make her way through the shelters and the streets. I kept my hair covered and wore baggy clothing. I pickpocketed to keep myself fed. I did a lot of running to keep away from certain groups of people. Sometimes I hitchhiked to a new city and started over."

"This is why you were so damn hard to find," Sol said with a shaky laugh. I smiled, relieved to see we were getting past the shock and sympathy. That was the worst part of having a rough past - the pity. All it did was make me feel broken again.

I wasn't fucking broken - I'd healed stronger.

"One night, I was rummaging through some trash at a festival, and a woman came up to me and offered me a meal and some money. She smelled nice and honest, and I'd learned to trust my power and my instincts, so I went with her to a diner. That was LuAnn."

Again, I ignored Killian's rough curse. "She wasn't perfect, but she did help keep me safe for a long time," I pointed out. "I think she felt sorry for me at first. As we talked over dinner, I decided to trust her, and I told her what I could do. She'd heard rumors of Underbelly and believed in stuff like magic. Over that first meal, we designed our future festival booth. I went back to her trailer, and she gave me a key. She promised I could leave any time - that made me trust her more. Over the summer, she let me practice my power on her. Once I got pretty good at drawing out emotions, our booth saw some success. LuAnn wasn't the family I'd hoped for, but I had food and safe shelter, even a little spending money."

"When did you come across the girl from Underbelly?" Jai asked, breaking his long silence.

I considered. "I'd been with LuAnn for about a year, I think. Sometimes we argued, and one night I was so angry I just left. That was the first time the girl found me. I didn't like the emotions she was putting off - she was lying a lot. I ended up going back to LuAnn, and I told her what had happened. She decided we should begin moving around even more often. We started tracking the Underbelly movements and sort of followed behind them.

She thought it was safer that way, because we'd always know where he was."

"I guess that was smart enough," Sol allowed.

I nodded. "It was the best we could do. Neither of us had the money or the knowledge to really get out of the country or start over completely somewhere. Running is all I've ever known."

Silence crept around the table as I stopped talking, and the guys all looked deep in thought.

"So, have I earned dessert?" I said hopefully, trying to break the tension in the room.

Jai and Sol chuckled, rising and beginning to clear the table of dirty dishes. Killian rolled his eyes, but he nodded to me as he stood up. I smiled back, thinking I must have earned a tiny bit of respect from him.

I looked to Dair, who hadn't moved yet.

"You do need training," he said, then lowered his voice and leaned close. "Because I don't want you to run anymore."

My chest grew tight as I took in the intensity of his navy eyes.

"I agree," Jai called from the sink. "Starting now, I want Sol to work on physical defense, Killian to check on her knife skills, and Dair to explain how magic works. We don't know how your power will manifest, so better to be prepared," he added, looking at me.

Murmurs of "yes, boss" circled the room.

"I'll take first shift," Killian said, surprising me. "On the deck, kiddo. Let's see how you throw."

My stomach flipped at the thought of training with Killian first, but maybe it *would* help if we got to know each other better. I stood and handed my plate to Sol, then followed Killian out the back door.

CHAPTER TWENTY

CARLYLE

I glanced over at the shattered section of deck railing. It was even weirder in broad daylight to think I'd crushed a plank of wood with my hands. Then again, everything was weird about my current situation, from the fact that I was living with a bunch of ancient magical dudes to the idea that I was about to start training for a freaking *mission* like some sort of secret agent.

Killian beckoned me farther down, choosing a spot away from any windows. The early afternoon air was warm, and a light breeze ruffled through the pine trees. I inhaled deeply, wishing the peaceful view would calm into my spinning thoughts.

"Sounds like you think you have some nice experience.

Care to show me what the lil lamb knows?" Killian taunted, totally ruining the peace.

I bit back a groan. Glancing over my shoulder, I saw him pull a switchblade from his pocket and begin flipping it around his fingers.

Flipping it in the air, he caught it easily. I watched for a few seconds, not too impressed. "I've hung around circus and festival people for years," I said. "It takes more than a few twists of the wrist to impress me."

Killian lifted his eyebrows in challenge, then he hurled the knife at my hand on the railing, where it thunked neatly into the wood barely an inch from my thumb.

"Asshole! What if I'd moved?"

He just shrugged, and anger started to simmer in me. I yanked his knife from the wood and imitated his complex flips and twirls, staring him down instead of watching the blade.

Killian rolled his eyes, his boredom a challenge.

I glared and scanned the wall behind his head, looking for a knothole to use as a target. I pointed to one with the tip, then flung the knife end over end until it met its appointed bullseye. Killian shrugged. He pulled the knife out of the wall, then picked out another knothole, farther away on the planking, and repeated the action. I noted the distance and matched it on my turn.

We traded throws like this for several minutes, each time getting higher and higher on the wall, until I couldn't reach the handle anymore.

"Not too bad, kid," Killian said. His voice was still pretty flat, though. I could tell he wasn't really that impressed. "But what about a moving target?"

I'd expected as much. "Well, how about you start

running, and I'll see if I can hit you?" I smiled, sweet as pie.

Killian's golden eyes sparked at me, and he ran his hand through his bright red hair in habit. He smirked and held out his hand. I drew in a sharp breath as a ball of light formed in his palm. It looked a little like a ball of fire, but it wasn't fire colored - more of a greenish brown.

I wondered briefly if it would burn me, but before I could ask, Killian launched it in the air with a flick of his wrist.

"Hit that, if ya can," he said.

The ball of light hovered in the air just above me for second, before slipping away into the trees, back and forth like a lightning bug. I watched its movement for several seconds, noticing how random its movement was. So much for impressing him.

"Any tips?" I asked, grudgingly.

"Consider this a placement test," he said with a snicker. "Now quit stalling and throw."

"Fuck off. Will the blade even stick in that thing?" I asked, totally stalling.

Killian stared at me, his lip curling. "Jus' throw. I can retrieve the knife after ya miss."

Ugh. He was impossible. Shading my eyes against the bright sun, I tried to focus on the greenish light flitting a few feet above me. Taking careful aim, I let go of the knife.

Killian chuckled as the blade sailed right over the ball of light into the woods beyond. He mumbled a few words, and the knife reappeared, floating toward us. He plucked it out of the air.

"I didna expect you to hit it."

"Thanks for the lesson, sensei," I retorted. "A randomized target isn't exactly fair, though. Even human behavior isn't really random. When you're fighting someone, you can find patterns in their movement."

"Only if you don't get knocked out before ya have a chance to study them," he pointed out.

"Plus, I can usually tell by a human's scent what emotion they're feeling. If they start to smell afraid, then I'm getting the upper hand in the fight. If they start to smell cocky, then they might be ready to mess up."

He frowned. "Problem is, kiddo, you won't be fighting many humans from now on." He handed the knife back to me. "Again."

I knew he was right. Gritting my teeth, I set aside my pride and got ready to learn. If I wanted to be part of the team, after all, I had to show I was willing to work with them. Killian had probably picked first shift on purpose, so he could brag about how lazy I was.

A few throws in, Killian actually began coaching me. He rambled on about wind direction and speed, finger pressure and hand-eye coordination. An hour later, my arm was aching from the repetitive throws, but then I hit the ball.

"Fuck yes!" I yelled, pumping my fist in the air. The ball exploded in tiny fireworks across the backyard, and the knife floated right back to rest on the railing.

I turned to Killian and actually caught the edge of a smile before he wiped it away.

He nodded and handed the knife back to me. "Now do it again, but with the opposite hand."

My jaw dropped. "Are you serious right now?"

He said nothing, folding his arms across his chest and

143

raising his stupid eyebrow again.

"Goddamn, I hate you," I muttered.

He snorted back a laugh, just as the sliding door opened on the other end of the deck, and Sol strode toward us with a shit-eating grin on his face.

"We're havin' a lesson here," Killian said dryly.

"Fuck that. I just asked Jai about how our girl here broke the railing yesterday, and he wants us all inside now."

My eyes widened, and I hurried past the two of them. This, I wanted to hear.

Jai and Dair were settled in the living room, and I curled myself onto the end of one of the long leather couches. Sol dropped in next to me, and Killian stood by the window again.

"So?" I asked, nearly bouncing in my seat in anticipation.

Jai cleared his throat delicately and looked around the circle until each of the guys had met his gaze. "The first thing I want to say is that Carlyle must *never* feel pressured to find or use her power. Qilin are to be respected and worshiped. Not used." His face twisted in disgust, and I wondered what he'd seen in the past to make him so harsh with his team. None of them had pressured me to do anything yet - not really. I knew I could walk away at any moment.

They all nodded solemnly, though.

Jai said, "Carlyle, you've been using your power most of your life without being aware of it. Humans do not possess real magic, but experiencing emotions is very close to a magical experience. After all, magic is - at its simplest - a change in our reality. As humans cycle through emotions, their reality changes."

I nodded, thinking I understood. "So, like when I pulled depression from people at festivals. For a while, their reality changed, because they were experiencing happiness."

"Very good," he said, nodding. "When you pull emotion from a human, you are practicing your Qilin power. If you were to accomplish the same thing with a Haretian, you would pull their magic instead."

He waited as the information settled in our brains. I wasn't quite sure what he meant, but Sol sat forward, his face open and excited as he stared at me.

"Your strength when you broke the railing... that was *my* strength," he gloated, and I gasped as Jai nodded.

"I took your magic?" I whispered. "But how? How was I strong enough?" Both Jack and Sol had said I was strong, but both had resisted me pulling anything from them.

"Think about what you were doing with our lion cub, just moments before you gained his strength," Dair suggested, his lips drawn up in a sexy smile.

"Doing? We... oh." I felt my face flush as my memories answered his question. Well, then. That would explain why Jai was so worried about me being pressured. I jerked to my feet and began pacing.

"So, when I, say, kiss someone from Haret, I can steal their power?" I turned my back to the guys. This was getting embarrassing. Not only was I a magical taxi cab, but apparently I was like one of those party busses with the black windows and a stripper pole inside.

Hop right in, and Carlyle will take you for a ride, then take your magic as payment.

Sol burst into laughter, and I whirled on him.

"Uh, that was funny?" he said, biting back another laugh.

"I said that out *loud*?" I screeched, yanking a pillow off a nearby chair and pressing it over my face. Fuck. I sank to the floor, wanting to keep sinking until I didn't have to look at any of them anymore.

"Carlyle, don't be embarrassed," Jai said, his voice low and careful. "You've lived your whole life in the human world. Humans love intimacy, but they also fear it because in their soul, it is tied to this same idea of exchanging magic. They demonize people - especially women - who seem to hold sexual power over others. But in Haret, these women are goddesses. These women are Qilin."

I heard his words, but my brain folded its arms like a stubborn child, refusing to listen.

A thud-click sounded on the floor, reaching me swiftly. Dair knelt on one knee beside me, and I felt his hand on my back, soft and soothing this time. "Carlyle, sweet, please listen to us. You may always say no to intimacy. But never feel shame in saying yes."

I let him stroke up and down my spine as I thought everything through. This idea was game-changing. I'd always hated and feared how my power seemed to make people go crazy with compounded emotion - until I learned to control and manipulate it.

If Jai was right, I could learn to do the same with magic. Now that would be real power.

With each second that ticked by, I began to dream of a world where desire was my weapon and my shield, rather than my Achilles' heel.

CHAPTER TWENTY-ONE

CARLYLE

Finally, I lifted my head and looked around the room. I met Dair's deep, navy blue eyes first. He met my gaze with heat, but also tenderness, and I melted enough to release my tightly-curled body. As I stood, I connected with Sol's gaze, and his smile was almost shy.

I smiled back, and his lips widened as my heart swelled.

Jai's black eyes caught mine just before he bowed his head deeply in a gesture of honor. Shock coursed through my body, and I stumbled. Dair's arm slipped around my waist, steadying me.

I looked at Killian last, and he smirked as usual, before turning his back to me and gazing out the ceiling-height window.

"How do you feel?" Sol asked, his voice cautious.

I narrowed my eyes. This reverence was actually weirder than pity over my past.

"Hungry for dessert," I offered, and the odd tension shattered with the now-familiar joke.

Killian groaned and sauntered toward the front door. "Always with the sugar. Maybe your Qilin form will be more like a rhino than a dainty white horse."

I laughed, unfazed. Nothing would ever keep me from sugar. "I'll be a fat fucking unicorn if I want to. I've spent way too many years of my life hungry, and if I want to lay my ears back, it's none of your goddamn business."

His eyes grew wide, and he choked on a laugh before slipping out the door. I heard an engine rev to life, and within seconds, that fancy-ass silver car was tearing down the winding driveway.

"Asshole," I muttered, turning back to others. I caught the edge of a look between Dair and Jai, but then Dair tugged me toward the kitchen.

"Lay your ears back?" Sol questioned as he followed, a smile playing across his lips.

"Southern expression," I replied. LuAnn was from Tennessee, and I'd picked up plenty of her funny sayings. "Like dig in and eat like crazy."

"Does this work?" Dair asked, as a white cardboard carton appeared on the counter, then a spoon. Like they were conjured from thin air.

"Ice cream?" I asked, lifting the lid.

"Gelato," he corrected, sampling it with the spoon I'd thought had been for me.

"And you just, what, made it? Can you create things?" I wondered. I eyed the spoon in his hand, but he only smiled and took another bite. I fought the urge to snatch the spoon from him.

"Dair has a talent for *procurement*," Sol answered, rolling his eyes.

"Procurement?" I repeated, catching Sol's snicker. He shrugged, pulling a bottle of beer from the fridge and settling at the table. I looked back at Dair. "So, finding things? Or is it more like stealing?" Here I'd pegged him for an uptight businessman. I wasn't sure how I felt about wearing stolen clothes. Or eating stolen gelato, if he ever gave me the chance.

He ate another bite, and I made a tiny groan of impatience.

"I'm especially good at spells that move items from one location to another. It comes in handy for all manner of jobs," Dair said, his lips twisting in a lethal grin. "Once I've seen and remembered something, I can call it to me with a bit of magic, as long as its location hasn't changed very much."

"Yeah, so watch those pants," Sol said, glowering at Dair as he tipped his bottle back. "He could magic them right off your legs."

Dair threw a sideways glance at Sol. "That hardly requires magic, cub."

"So you just magically stole that carton of gelato? *And* my outfit?" I wanted to be clear on this before I decided how I felt. "What about the people you steal from?"

He shrugged. "I buy plenty of things, too. I only take from those who have more than enough." He raised a brow in challenge, and I flushed. I wasn't exactly innocent when it came to stealing, either, and I always justified it the same way.

He dug the spoon into the carton and finally offered the bite to me. I hesitated, preferring not to be fed. He pulled the spoon back a bit. I thought he was going to eat the bite again, so I leaned forward, opening my mouth. He smiled, all victorious and shit. I would have probably protested, but the cool creamy sweetness spread over my tongue, and a tiny moan slipped out.

Okay, I didn't care if it was stolen. This gelato stuff was a slice of heaven.

Dair waited until I swallowed before spooning up a second bite. He held the spoon out again, but I had to lean a little farther forward to reach it this time. I knew what he was doing, but the gelato was so good I really didn't care.

By the fourth bite, I was practically in his lap, and Sol banged out of the kitchen onto the back deck, leaving us alone.

I scooted back in my chair, huffing. "I'm sorry, but I can't do this to him," I muttered, trying to ignore the next offered bite.

"You're doing nothing," Dair said, his voice dark and steely. "Sol's jealousy stems from himself - never from you."

I shook my head. "He's been nothing but sweet. I shouldn't be flirting with you after we…"

Dair fixed his deep blue eyes on me, waiting for me to continue. I hesitated.

"Have you made him a promise to be only with him?" he asked when I didn't continue.

"No," I said, a wry smile creeping onto my lips. The way LuAnn and I had moved around, I'd never seen any guy more than a day or two. "I don't know much about dating, but I'm pretty sure that if you want to keep seeing someone, that sort of promise is inevitable."

"Ah," he said, leaning back in his chair and propping his ankle on his knee. I took the opportunity to grab the carton and spoon, and he snickered. "Do you want to keep seeing Sol?"

I knew my cheeks must be as red as the tomato sauce from dinner, but I nodded. I really liked Sol. I didn't want to mess it up.

"You know, many races in Haret are polyamorous in one way or another. Qilin females often have multiple partners at once, though the males tend to prefer a single female Qilin."

I frowned, setting the gelato aside. "How does that work, then?"

"Females who aren't interested in bearing children typically collect their men from whichever races they prefer."

I giggled as my mind raced to the gutter. This house already held quite the collection of men. I shook away the idea as fast as it had come. I'd never dated anyone, so it was probably better to start slow.

"Thank you for the gelato," I said instead of asking him the dozen questions popping into my mind.

"Of course, Cariño." He captured my fingers, and that same electric spark crackled up my wrist as he pressed his lips briefly to my palm. My fingers curled around his jaw before I drew my hand back and fled the room, heading upstairs to my bedroom.

Shit, it was going to be hard to control my desire around Dair. He seemed to be constantly pushing without being pushy, and it made my head spin.

CHAPTER TWENTY-TWO

CARLYLE

As soon as I opened the door to my room, though, I saw Dair reclining on my bed.

"What-how-" I spluttered, and he only shrugged.

"Magic, of course."

"Of course." I threw my hands up. I mean, yes, of course it was magic. What I really wanted to ask him was why he was in my room.

"I could leave you alone, but we're in a bit of a hurry, sweet. I thought I might as well teach you how magic works to distract you from worrying your pretty head about Sol."

I sank onto the bed at his feet, which were still in boots. On my white bedspread.

"I don't want to cause trouble between you guys," I muttered.

Dair narrowed his eyes and sat up slowly. He leveled his gaze with mine. "You would not be the cause. If Sol is jealous, then he is the cause of his own jealousy. You've made him no promises," he repeated.

"What if I do, though? What if I promise him he's the only one for me? Will you stop flirting with me?" I challenged.

Dair's eyes flashed. "If you did indeed mate and make an exclusive life-bond with my brother, I would honor it without question." The corner of his lip twisted up. "Something tells me you're just not ready to mate for eternity."

I gaped. Nope. Those words were definitely not on my list of things to say or do. Mating? Gross - it still sounded like animals. Eternity? Hell to the no.

"Wait. How long do Qilin live?" I asked.

"When Haret was healthy, all its races enjoyed lifespans of nearly a thousand years. When I was born, that had already shortened to half. I don't know how much worse it's gotten since the Path collapsed."

I picked at some fuzz on the blanket, still very uncomfortable being the last hope of a dying world.

"Here," Dair said, holding out a steaming mug that had most definitely not been in his hands a moment ago. He took a sip, grimacing. "Disgusting."

I took the cup and tasted the sweetened coffee, a grin spreading over my face. "Perfect."

"Well, then, drink up while I begin my demonstration." Dair flicked his fingers at my rumpled clothes, still on the floor. They floated up and into the bathroom. He moved his hand again, and the bathroom door shut. "Manipulating nearby objects is among the simplest of spells."

"But your talent at *procurement* is much more advanced, right?" I teased.

The corners of his mouth quirked up. "Precisely. Now, nearly all mages are born with a basic level of magic within them, the way most humans are born with the ability to learn to walk and run. Training and practice help in both examples, as do certain techniques, equipment, and supplements."

"So, like a marathoner would have special shoes and a diet and exercise plan, you have something like that, too?" I asked, appreciating the comparison.

He nodded. "A mage often uses an object infused with magic to help intensify his skill. This is where the idea of a magic wand came about, as sticks are relatively easy to find and small enough to keep on hand. The objects do need to be something of the elements, though. I prefer precious metals and stones over sticks." He held up his arm and pointed to the crisp cuff of his button-up shirt. His cufflink was silver, set with a dark, sparkling stone. Pushing up his sleeve, he showed me a thick-banded watch inset with more of the black stones, as well as square-cut diamonds.

"Nice," I murmured. The mage business must pay well, unless he'd stolen all of that, too.

"Are you wondering about procurement?" he asked, settling back against the headboard.

I shrugged, keeping my eyes on the bottom of my coffee cup as I drained it.

"When we were sent here from Haret, we were given

154

more than enough human funding to ensure we wouldn't have to steal. I only procure items for convenience. I also help our kind whenever I find them here on Earth - they're trapped here as well, remember. Sometimes they choose to pay me. So you may enjoy your lace panties with a clear conscience."

There was a bit of a mocking edge to his voice, and I decided to stop questioning him about where things came from. Honestly, I didn't care as much as he thought I did, as long as he wasn't hurting people who needed the money. "What about supplements?" I asked, changing the topic. "Eye of newt, and all that."

"Some mages practice in potions, which use all sorts of odd ingredients. I've never had much patience for that sort of thing. My natural talents lie in the manipulation of matter - that's an earth-based magic. I also hold a special interest in the power of language, and how it affects the physical world around us."

"What does that mean?" Sure, power of the pen and all, but he'd lost me.

"Going back to our marathoner example, he might repeat a mantra or affirmation to convince himself to keep running. Those words have a power for him. Names have immense power, because they are integrated with our sense of who we are."

"What does Carlyle Licorne mean to your magic?" I'd looked up my name online before, but I wanted to hear his take on it.

Dair's deep blue eyes widened, and he suddenly looked much younger in his excitement. "Your last name is Licorne? And still you resist our claim on you?"

My cheeks flushed. "First of all, you *have* no claim on

me. But no, I'm not really resisting anymore." My voice trailed away as I admitted that even though it still sounded crazy, the probability of me being their lost Qilin was pretty damn high.

"*Licorne* is the French word for unicorn," he said, and I nodded. I'd been ignoring this fact for a few days now, but I couldn't really explain it as coincidence any longer. "Carlyle has a long history, and it's more often a name given to a male. This may be why it took us so long to locate you. One powerful meaning for it is 'one who desires freedom'. This desire makes up part of your very soul, doesn't it?"

I looked up and met his gaze, and I felt he could see the truth of his words, all the way down into that same soul. "Is that a Qilin story?"

"Absolutely," he whispered. "Which leaves only one to test."

"One?" I echoed. Surely there were more theories. Surely I hadn't proved so easily that I was a Qilin, without even a single scrap of magic to show.

"Only one serious one. The ability to shift into your true form."

I flopped back on the bed, staring at the ceiling. I'd been joking about being a fat unicorn. Or even a rhino.

"I'm not sure I want to be a shifter. I like my body."

Dair's smooth movements brought him close in an instant, his chest pressed along my side as he propped up his elbow. "I like your body, too, Cariño," he said, his other hand coming to rest on my stomach.

I pushed him back a few inches. "You know what I mean. I don't want to be a horse."

He chuckled. "Qilin are not horses. Unicorns and Qilin

share some characteristics, but unicorns are the human version. Less powerful. Less frightening."

"What does a Qilin look like, then?"

"Every Qilin is different. Killian's second sight can only see a blurred version of your final form. Your specific appearance will be a reflection of the magic you claim. Some Qilin do have white hides like the myth of the unicorn, but many are covered in fur, leathery armor, and even scales."

"Really?" That would be pretty badass, actually. Much better than the dainty, sparkling creatures I'd seen in posters and all over little girls' stuff in the stores. Way cooler than the chubby, rainbow-farting ones that had gotten popular, too.

"Some Qilin do have a single horn, but some have two, or even four. Some have manes and tails like horses, and some look more like lions."

I smiled to myself, picturing a creature with a majestic lion's mane and gorgeous, shimmery scales. It seemed to suit me better than a delicate, dreamy thing made of glitter and marshmallows.

"So how do I shift?" I asked.

"I have no fucking clue," Dair said, and I giggled.

CHAPTER TWENTY-THREE

CARLYLE

Dair worried the edge of the pillowcase, picking at a loose thread.

"Growing up the way you did, it's a miracle you avoided the Ringmaster - or someone just as corrupt - as long as you did." His voice was soft, though a hint of anger had seeped into his calm tone.

"How did he get your friend?" I asked, suddenly needing to know every detail of Jack's capture. If it had happened to him…

Dair's jaw tensed, and he stared beyond the window into the woods. He was silent long enough that I didn't think he would answer. Then, "I wish I knew."

"We'll get him back," I said, and his eyes slid back to

mine. "Now tell me how to steal your spells."

His sensual lips turned up at my suggestion, and my heart beat faster. I wasn't sure I was ready to sidetrack this teacher with kisses even though a certain part of me was already pulsing with anticipation.

"According to Jai, magic is harder to pull and push than strength or human emotion, but the principle should be the same - you get my spells with touch." His smile widened, and I felt my cheeks heat.

"Well, fuck," I murmured. There went that resolution. Of course, there were plenty of ways to touch him without being sexual. I would totally focus on those. Totally.

"So, are you going to try or not?" Dair prompted, staring down at me as I lay on my back. My heart began to beat double-time. Surely I didn't need to kiss him for this. Even though Dair had tried to reassure me I could do what I wanted, he was kind of like the big bad wolf telling me why his ears were so big. I still wanted to clear the air with Sol before anything more happened.

I sat up, and Dair followed, so we were facing each other on my bed. This felt less intimate than lying next to each other, and relief slowed my galloping Qilin heart. He held out his hands, and I rested mine in them, palm to palm. His long fingers closed over my wrists in tight circles. I bit back a hiss, but I didn't pull away.

"Now, close your eyes and try to feel the magic when I use it," he instructed.

I did as he requested, my senses hyper-aware of touching him even this much. His scent filled my nose - the sweet musk of pipe tobacco, cut through with the brightness of champagne. I'd had champagne exactly once in my life, and I'd never forgotten its tangy sweet bite against my tongue.

My palms tingled a tiny bit, and my eyes flew open. Dair clicked his tongue at me, shaking his head.

"So disobedient. Did you feel something?"

"Maybe," I answered. "What did you do?"

He nodded to the bedside table, where I'd set my empty mug. It was filled again, steaming with fresh coffee. "Procured from the kitchen - not stolen," he teased.

"Again," I said, closing my eyes.

We repeated the action dozens of times, each time Dair fetching something small or moving an object around the room with his magic. I was soon able to correctly tell him if he had used magic or not each time he asked.

"I'm very impressed," he murmured finally, withdrawing his fingers from mine. I felt the loss of his touch like a hollow spot in my heart, and my body's reaction scared me a little.

"We started small," I said, shrugging. "My power may not be that strong."

"Starting small proved your power," Dair contradicted. "It wouldn't be hard at all to detect me using large quantities of magic. Even normal humans can often feel a change in the air or see a flash of magic that they interpret as light or a trick of their peripheral vision. But for you to feel something as tiny as me moving a pillow - Carlyle, you're incredibly strong."

I smiled up at him, feeling suddenly shy. "You're the third person to tell me that now. I just feel so… so *unable*."

His hand stretched toward me, ghosting over my cheek and jaw before falling to his lap. "You will learn, Cariño. We will teach you everything we can, but you'll learn faster if you listen to the needs of your heart and your body."

Heat pooled deep in my core at his words and the cool absence left after his caress.

Heavy footsteps sounded in the hallway then, and I quickly sat back against the headboard. Sol's giant frame filled the doorway, and he grinned at me, pointedly ignoring Dair.

"In bed again? I came to see if you wanted to do something more active."

"Sure," I said, returning his smile while trying to ignore Dair's intense gaze. I scooted off the bed and stretched. It would be nice to move around, actually.

"Our little Qilin has come far today," Dair said. "But she feels like she needs permission to go further. Have you led her to believe she needs yours?" His tone had grown icy, and I snapped my eyes back to his face.

"What are you talking about?" I demanded. "Sol hasn't, like, *claimed* me or anything."

"Funny," Sol said, his tone without humor. "*Claiming* is just another word for *fucking*. Right, mage?" He spun on his heel and was gone before I could react. I heard a door slam somewhere beyond.

"Such a temper in the cub," Dair said, disdain obvious on his beautiful face.

"Why did you ask him that?" I stood, glaring down at him. "What good did it do to taunt him?"

Dair rose, his body now looming dangerously close to mine. "He needs to be reminded that no matter what word he uses, Qilin get what Qilin want. And Qilin females always want more than one cock."

Heat flared from him, and on instinct, I nearly reached for his hips to pull him closer. Instead, I clenched my hands into fists at my side and stared sideways out into the hallway.

Dair stepped back again, leaving me missing his warmth. "You don't have to choose, Cariño," he whispered, then disappeared before my eyes, the air popping against my skin.

"Ugh," I cried, reaching across the bed and hurling a pillow against the wall. Who needed magic? "Fucking men!"

"You rang?" The words drawled out in an unmistakably sarcastic voice.

"What do *you* want?" I growled at Killian.

"Well, I am a man. And while I'm not fuckin' anyone at the moment, I like to leave my options open." He leaned against the wall as I rolled my eyes. At least I didn't have to worry about Killian coming on to me. He alternated between thinking I was an idiot or a child. "Did you run off lion boy? I was hoping to do a little sparring."

"Sorry to inconvenience you," I muttered.

He took a step into the room, claiming my attention. "I know ya were raised human, but get over it, kid. Haretians play ball with different rules. Qilin especially. So fuck Sol if ya want. Fuck Dair, too. Hell, I bet even Jack would go for ya if we can get his fuckin' brain back. Nobody cares."

I glared at him. "Sol obviously does. He threw a goddamn hissy fit just now and stormed off because of Dair."

Killian laughed, tipping his head back in true mirth. "Fuckin' hell. I missed it?" He barked another loud laugh. "Shit, girl. You must give it good." He circled his hips in a lewd motion, and I threw the other pillow at him.

"Fuck off."

"Seriously. Dair can be an asshole, but Sol is na' usually

the jealous type. We even share a girl sometimes," he said, rubbing his fingers over his flame-stubbled jaw.

"Share?" I gaped at him. As in…

A wicked grin spread across his face, and I was reminded again of the first time I'd seen him - when I'd been locked in that powerful gaze from across a street.

"Yeh, share. I call it a fuck an' suck." With a cackle, he sauntered away, leaving me staring open-mouthed after him, my mind going a mile a minute trying to imagine just what he meant. Possibilities flew through my head, leaving me breathless and way, way too curious to see if I was right.

Ah, hell. These Haret men were going to be the death of me.

KILLIAN

I waited until I was safe in my room before dialing Sol's cell. The fucker needed a thrashing.

"What?" Sol growled as the call connected.

"Why are you being such a dick about the kid?" I asked him bluntly.

"Not you, too," Sol groaned. "Jai already gave me the look when I left."

"Because you're bein' such a human about it. She already feels guilty because of all that fucked-up shit from her past. Donna make it worse."

"Yeah? Why do you care? You treat her like she's twelve, not twenty-one."

I swore under my breath, trying really goddamn hard to

keep my temper. "Quit changin' the topic like a little bitch. Handle your shit, come home, and apologize to Carlyle. This is our way home, Sol. Donna fuck it up."

I ended the call before Sol could say another word and chucked the phone on the bed. I felt sorry for the girl, but there was no way I was going to let emotions into play here.

She might be the best lay in both worlds, but if she couldn't find the Path, I would lose everything I'd worked for in Haret.

We'd all volunteered for this mission for different reasons, but I was beginning to think I was the only one who remembered just what was at stake here.

We were almost out of time, and that crazy fuckin' Ringmaster was getting stronger every goddamn day we wasted.

CHAPTER TWENTY-FOUR

CARLYLE

I was bouncing with nervous energy after all that male posturing bullshit, so I quickly changed into a pair of workout shorts and a loose tank top. I bound my pale hair up in a tight braid, then explored the house until I found the empty workout room all the way in the basement.

One wall was lined with racks of free weights and a large mirror, and the other had a short row of treadmills. A blue mat spread across the middle of the floor, and a cabinet I opened held a variety of gloves. There was even a new punching bag in the corner. I wondered if Killian would come down to work out without Sol, but I pushed the thought away. It didn't matter who came down here - I had every right to burn off some frustration.

I stepped onto one of the treadmills, mainly because it was the only thing in the room I really knew how to use. It wasn't like I'd ever been privileged enough to go to a gym.

Fifteen minutes into my light jog, I heard steps on the stairs, and Sol appeared.

"Hey," he said, sounding a little embarrassed.

"Come to teach me to fight?" I turned off the treadmill and smiled, hoping to just brush past all the awkwardness.

"Definitely," he grinned, looking relieved.

He walked me through several basic self-defense moves, and I was grateful to see that, even though I was rusty as shit, I still had a good foundation.

"Ready for the next level, then?" he asked as we took a quick break and grabbed cold water bottles from a mini fridge in the corner.

I shrugged, but my stomach flipped. I was much more comfortable with knives than fists.

Thirty minutes later, I was so regretting ever being nice to Sol. "Are you teaching me to fight or to fall?" I growled as my back hit the mat again. It wasn't as hard as the floor, but shit, it was beginning to sting. Time after time, he'd set me up, move my limbs around in a mimicry of a fight, and then he'd pull some bitch move and knock me over.

He was quickly losing his status as my favorite and moving right into asshole territory with Killian.

"Falling is a skill in fighting. You can prevent a lot of injuries by falling correctly. Now, up. Again," he demanded.

Grumbling to myself, I hauled my body up again, assuming the stance.

The afternoon wore on, and eventually I began to notice some repetition in his extra moves. Patterns started to click into place, and my muscles found their power in a few moves.

Pretending I was on a city street, I walked the width of the basement as instructed. He darted out from the shadows, grabbing me around the waist from behind. My feet dangled off the floor, and my training kicked in as I lifted my knees to my chest and shoved my heels back viciously into his padded groin. The movement doubled him, breaking his arm hold, and I braced my arms before me as I fell, hitting the mat and rolling into a crouch.

He straightened and came at me, leaning down and raising his fist to show how easily he could punch me in the temple. Instead of conceding defeat, though, I twisted and shot to my feet, smacking his arm away with one hand and using the heel of the other hand to smash up into his nose.

"Fuck," he cursed in admiration, as a bright spot of blood dripped from one nostril. I grinned, not feeling one bit guilty.

I knew a real fight likely wouldn't give me the time to pull that move, but I was still proud of how far I'd come in an afternoon. Pinching the bridge of his nose to staunch the tiny bit of blood, Sol lifted the edge of his shirt to wipe it away.

I totally tried not to stare at his bare abs, and I totally failed. Goddamn lion was ripped.

Probably, he'd knocked a few girls unconscious just by flexing those abs.

"Nice job," he said, his voice muffled as he pulled the bloodied shirt over his head, balling it up and chucking it into the corner. All that golden, velvety skin shone with a fine layer of sweat, and I had to turn my back on the pretense of getting some water.

I mean, yeah, I was parched, but no amount of H20 was going to solve this draught.

"Again," he said, and I gritted my teeth, forcing myself to turn back to his bare chest and repeat the sequence several more times. We practiced the identical moves in slow-motion to cement them in my muscle memory.

Or so he said, but each repetition got suspiciously less like a fight.

Before long, we weren't fighting so much as performing a violent sort of dance, my fingernails scraping against his bare shoulder, his palms sliding along my slick neck, and our eyes locking at every turn like they were heat magnets. But I wasn't complaining - instead of the blunt sting of hitting the mat, I was treated to the low burn of his fingers.

His deep chocolate eyes promised so much more than a fighting lesson, but he kept his hands stubbornly to the prescribed moves, and the rest of my body raged with neglect. Ever since the argument with Dair, he'd seemed determined not to do anything with me that might come within a hundred miles of either claiming or fucking.

Our lesson was quickly devolving into a battle of wills, and I wanted to see his control break.

I wanted to be the one to break him.

So, the next time he grabbed me from behind, I didn't fight back like I was supposed to. Instead, I arched my ass into his groin, snatching his hands from my waist and tugging them up to palm my breasts.

His breath hitched, and I let my head fall back against his chest, rolling my hips back against him.

I was so fucking tired of resisting my desires and trying

to consider how everything might affect the team. I'd had a rough few days, and come hell or high water, I was having this man.

"Damn, shortcake," he said, his chest heaving. His hands cupped around the fullness of my breasts, his thumbs brushing over the hard peaks of my nipples, and I moaned. God, I needed this shirt and bra off, now.

So help me, if he didn't have a condom, I was going to kill him.

I twisted in his grasp and shoved him back the few steps to the wall. His hands jerked down to my hips, and several fingers slid beneath the hem of my shirt, gliding up my spine. His sunshine and warm grass smell swirled around us, and I grinned at him.

I loved my power when it showed me gorgeous emotions like this.

I reached up and pulled his head down, tangling my fingers in his dark blond waves and pressing my lips against his. He answered with a groan, opening my lips with his. His tongue stroked hard and commanding against mine.

I straddled his thigh, pressing closer and rubbing my palms across his hard muscle, exploring every dip and ridge. His hand slid down over the curve of my ass and locked on the top of my thigh, fingers stretching between us to knead the sensitive skin at the edge of my panties.

His teeth grazed along my jaw and nipped at my earlobe, and my breath hitched. I shifted and rolled my hips again, the movement pushing his fingers past the lace and toward my center.

"Not so fast," he murmured, taking his lips away from me. He even drew his hand off my thigh, resting it back on my waist, and I whimpered in frustration. He kissed lightly down my throat, pausing to suck gently at the curve of my collarbone. "I like a bit of sugar before my sex."

Oh my god, the man was going to kill me.

I just wanted him to slam me to the stars, and here he was talking about sugar.

CHAPTER TWENTY-FIVE

CARLYLE

Still intent on being the one in control, Sol swiveled us with a quick movement. Now, I was the one pinned against the concrete wall. He stretched both of my hands above my head, grasping my wrists in one hand. I stared up at him, undecided whether to fight for my control back or just wait to see what he had in mind. He tilted the rest of his body away, leaving me with just a view.

I fidgeted against the wall, impatient, as his eyes raked slowly over my curves. I was in simple athletic shorts and a tank, basic cotton bra beneath. Not the sexiest thing, but the way he was staring made me feel like a pin-up girl. I smiled in what I hoped was a come-hither sort of way.

He leaned forward and pressed a chaste kiss on my lips.

I tried to tease him in for more, but he pulled away and waited for me to still.

"Good," he murmured as I pressed myself against the cold cement wall. His eyes were heavy-lidded.

So, that was the game. I could fucking play, too. He leaned in for another kiss, and I kicked my legs up and around his waist, locking my ankles behind his back before he could back away.

"Good," I mimicked, drawing him closer until his cock pressed hard against my clit through our shorts. I rolled my hips against him, doing the teenager dry-fuck like a pro. His eyes rolled back, and his arm muscles strained as he pushed his other hand against the wall.

"You win," he said, letting go of my wrists. His voice was husky and raw, his eyes a dark inferno.

He slid a hand behind my arching back and yanked at the elastic of my shorts, pulling them and my panties down in one violent movement. I unwrapped my legs just long enough to kick away the clothes, then lifted my body back to his. I clutched his broad shoulders, kneading at the bunched muscle. His hand slipped beneath my ass, pressing my hips into his.

"Condom?" I managed, a second before he slipped a thick finger inside me, pumping slowly a few times.

My thoughts scattered, but Sol didn't let me down.

"Haretians don't have human sickness," he whispered, his breath hot on my neck as our hips rocked. I breathed in deep and smelled nothing but truth and hot, hot need. I darted out my tongue to taste the salty sweetness of his golden skin.

"Qilin can only become pregnant with other Qilin." He added a second finger, and I cried out.

That was amazing as fuck - all of it, not just the blessed fingers. I'd always been doubly careful with my one-night stands, but the idea of feeling every inch of that golden man inside me had me writhing against him. I was frantic for more.

"Please," I whispered, losing the last of my dignity. Two fingers weren't enough.

A growl rumbled through his chest, and he finally released my wrists, both hands sliding beneath my ass to hold me up. I reached between us to shove down his shorts, getting my first look.

Fucking hell. And I thought his abs were impressive.

"Gimme," I said, grinning and stroking along his thick shaft. His eyes fluttered closed, and he dropped his mouth to my shoulder, muffling a groan. I drew the head of his cock slowly through my folds, circling his velvety tip around my clit a couple of times before positioning him right at my entrance.

I tilted my hips, and he pushed in, the progress excruciatingly slow. I was grateful, though. It had been a long fucking time.

"Fuck, you're so tight," he groaned, once he was fully seated. I arched my back, relishing the sensation of being completely full. This was exactly what I needed. Pushing my hips up, I wiggled against him, encouraging him to get moving. He drew out nearly to the tip, then looked me right in the eyes and slammed all the way back in.

I cried out, my nails digging into his sides, pushing back into him to let him know he'd better fucking do that again.

"Glory be, fuck," I panted as he built up a torturous rhythm of slow out and fast in. Bastard was getting his goddamn foreplay even while we were fucking.

He knew what he was doing, though, and I began to feel the pressure build. Using his thrusting to pin me against the wall, he looped my arms around his neck and yanked the neck of my tank down, dropping his mouth to my breasts. His tongue sucked my hard nipple, then he bit just enough to make me groan for more.

"Goddamn tease," I huffed, pulling his mouth up to mine. I kissed him like I fucking owned him, and he finally rewarded me by speeding up. I lifted one leg above his shoulder and hooked my ankle around his neck, showing off.

"Fuck, shortcake, that's so hot." He growled, driving into me. The new angle pushed his cock tight against my G-spot, and I yelled out his name as he fucked me so fast I lost my breath.

His thumb slid around and pressed hard on my clit, and I shattered around him, my hips bucking as the most intense release I'd ever had swept through me. He ground his hips against mine, and I dug my fingernails into his shoulders as he spilled into me with a delicious lion's roar.

His thrusts took several seconds to slow, and aftershocks rode through my body in mind-numbing waves. His thumb tweaked my clit one last time, and I gasped and jerked at the sensitivity. He grinned and leaned down to kiss me once more, his hand sliding my legs gently down to the floor.

My knees felt like jelly, and I tightened my arms around his neck to keep from toppling over.

"You're a goddess," he whispered, gathering my body to his. His hands gentled as they stroked my bare skin, skimming over the curve of my hips and resting at my waist.

I felt my skin flush. For some reason, the compliment made me more self-conscious than what we'd just done. His words suddenly made our sex more than fucking, and that made me hella nervous, because I'd never had anything more.

If this was what claiming felt like, I just might be up for it. I didn't want to admit it, but I was falling hard for what this group had.

"Wanna test your strength?" Sol asked, giving me a cheeky grin as he tossed me a towel to clean up with, then my clothes.

My eyes widened. "Um, yeah! Wait... did you do that just to see my power?"

He was on me in a second, his lips covering mine as his hands cupped my chin sweetly.

"Never think that, Carlyle. Never."

The kiss grew hotter as he pressed me into the wall again, but after a few minutes, I pushed him away, panting but impatient. I wanted to see if I had stolen any of his magical lion strength. He grinned as I strode to the wall of free weights.

Checking out the numbers on each hunk of metal, I chose enough to equal my body weight. Sol slid them onto the bar for me.

Curling my fingers around it, I braced to lift - and hurled it across the room. It smashed into the opposite wall, narrowly missing a treadmill.

"Holy fuck," Sol said as we blinked at each other. "Guys!" he roared up the stairs.

CHAPTER TWENTY-SIX

CARLYLE

Dair was the first to arrive in the basement, actually using the stairs this time instead of popping my eardrums.

His observant eyes lingered over my swollen lips and Sol's mussed hair and shirtless chest. "Well, that story certainly isn't true," the mage drawled, leaning against the mirror.

"What story?" I asked.

Dair smirked, saying nothing. He'd taken off his jacket and vest, looking slightly more casual in only light gray slacks and a black button-up. The collar hung unbuttoned, and his sleeves were rolled to the elbows, exposing his chunky gold watch.

"What story?" I turned to Sol.

"Uh… innocence, I guess." He shuffled against the wall, his cheeks showing a slight flush beneath his tan. He reached for his water bottle and hid behind a long drink.

"Innocence?" My eyes narrowed at Dair. He winked, his gaze sweeping down my curves, and it clicked. "Ah. Like how unicorns are this symbol of purity and goodness and shit. You thought I would be a prissy, prudish virgin, didn't you?"

Sol spit water behind me, but the heat in Dair's midnight eyes kept me captured, everything else fading away.

"The second I saw you, I knew you weren't innocent," Dair whispered, coming off the wall and slinking toward me. "And I thanked the fucking gods."

"Why?" I murmured, my body drawing closer to his, too, as though I were being reeled in.

Sol cleared his throat with a growly sort of cough, and I blinked away from Dair. My cheeks felt warm, and I lowered my eyes. Shit. Barely ten minutes ago, I'd been wrapped around Sol's naked body, worrying about upsetting their group dynamic, and now I was basically jumping into Dair's arms.

I took several steps back, trying to clear my head.

Unfortunately, I ran straight into another hard male body, and my balance teetered sideways. A strong hand wrapped my waist, steadying me.

"Watch it, kiddo," Killian said, his voice rough. He let me go, and I scooted out of the way as Jai came silently down the stairs. His black eyes went immediately to the weight I'd flung across the room.

"By the moons of Haret," he whispered, causing Dair and Killian to follow his gaze.

"What happened there?" Killian asked.

"Ah. Seems I'm pretty strong now," I said, cocking an eyebrow.

"Fuck," Killian said, finally seeming impressed.

"Precisely," Dair smirked, and I tossed my water bottle at him. It smacked into his chest like it weighed ten pounds, and he doubled over in surprise.

"Shit! Sorry," I said, grimacing.

There was a beat of silence, then all the guys seemed to be scrambling to test my newfound strength. They gave me task after task, piling more weight on the bar and showing me different positions to test leg strength, too.

Our excitement was relatively short-lived, though, as my strength started to seep away. Soon, I could barely lift the empty bar.

"So it's temporary." I tried not to feel disappointed.

"That means more recharge sessions," Sol joked.

I huffed. "Fun, but pretty inconvenient, really."

Jai watched me from his perch on the stairs, his fingers tugging at his sparse beard.

"What are you thinking, boss?" I called, and his grin took me by surprise. He hid it quickly as the others glanced to him.

"I'm thinking you're right. We're still missing a piece of the puzzle. The Qilin of old had immense power. This strength you possessed wasn't truly yours. It was channeled, perhaps, while your bodies were joined. Once the connection broke, the power drained away again."

"Sounds like Carlyle may need to invest some time into experimentation," Dair said, dragging his eyes across my body.

"Perhaps some time in a shower, too," Killian added,

replacing the last weight and starting up the stairs. He looked pointedly back at Sol. "Oh, an' this house has plenty of *separate* showers, Solomon."

I flushed at his words. Asshole. Yeah, I did need a shower, but there was no need to make a big deal out of what had happened between Sol and me, especially after telling me to fuck anyone I wanted.

"Fine," I yelled up the stairs after Killian. "But it's your turn to make dinner."

Sol laughed, and I even caught a tiny smirk on Jai's face before he followed Killian up. Every time I saw boss man vampire smile, I wanted to make it happen again.

He had this calm, sensei vibe about him, where he seemed all ageless and wise. As soon as those full lips and smooth gaze cracked - even a smidge - he took my breath away. I started up the stairs, wondering what sort of power I might get from Jai, if I ever got close enough to steal a kiss.

When I got upstairs, I found that Killian's idea of making dinner was apparently dumping everything for sandwiches onto the table.

I made up a plate and carried it upstairs to my room, dutifully heading to take a shower. I did need one. Sex without condoms was, ah, messy, and so was lifting weights afterward.

When I finally turned off the water and padded back into my room, my bed held a pair of pale yellow silk pajamas that I guessed Dair had swiped from some unlucky store owner. Whatever - they felt yummy against my skin.

Snuggled under the covers, I admired the view of moon and stars and pointy treetops. My eyes grew heavy, sliding closed as my muscles relaxed, although unfortunately, my mind continued to pulse with questions.

What seemed like hours later, I was struggling to actually sleep. My body had rested, but my mind refused to settle.

Sighing, I gave up and pushed away the blankets. Maybe I'd check the freezer downstairs for a little more gelato. I padded my way through the dark, quiet house, but before I reached the kitchen, the blue glow of a computer screen drew me into the living room.

"Hello, Carlyle."

I heard Jai's soft voice before his face popped up from behind the laptop screen. He sat on the floor, his back against the couch and his computer on the low coffee table. I slid onto the couch behind him, itching to undo his tight bundle of hair and run my fingers through it.

I wanted to mess it up and see what happened.

"Are you getting any closer to finding Jack or the Ringmaster?" I asked, tucking my fingers under my legs.

He glanced over his shoulder at me and nodded. "Killian was able to place a magical tracker of sorts on Jack before he fled. It's been cleared and destroyed by now, but we got a general location first. It was very near one of the suspected circus camps."

"Why would Jack be working for him? And what about Toro - what exactly does it mean to go rogue?"

Jai tilted his head back on my cushion, massaging his temples lightly. "Going rogue is our catch-all phrase for whenever the human world catches up to us. The longer we're away from Haret - and each other - the weaker our minds grow. It's one of the main reasons we have regular check-ins during our missions. Toro was fine at the last one, but Jack… Jack's been missing for six cycles."

"How long is a cycle?" I asked, afraid to know how long Jack had been a prisoner of Underbelly.

"A year." Jai's answer was laced with sadness for his friend, and I sucked in a breath. That was a long time to be separated from the ones who cared about you. It also didn't bode well for our success.

"The Ringmaster must be insanely strong to hold and hide him that long."

"Mmm," Jai agreed, tapping out something on his laptop. I couldn't make sense of anything on his screen - it was just long lines of code. A few seconds passed in silence, as I didn't want to interrupt him. "How did your training go with Dair?" he asked, the tapping pausing again.

"Ah," I stalled. "I have a lot to learn." I wasn't sure my nerves could take it if Dair and I ended up in bed together. Not that Sol and I had needed a bed…

"You know much already, though," Jai said, interrupting my rambling thoughts. I narrowed my eyes at him, wondering if he was mocking me.

"I feel like I know nothing."

He nodded and pushed the laptop away, twisting to face me better. "Yet, Qilin are not known to be concerned with knowledge."

I frowned - had he just called me an airhead?

"You misunderstand," he said, lifting his hand to rest on mine. The scent of warm red wine, sea, and cool steel filled my lungs. I felt the simple honesty in his words. "Qilin are emotional creatures. They learn by feeling, not hearing or seeing. Being without your natural ability has made you uncertain of yourself, but with touch restored, you know, don't you?"

I took a few beats to process his words, but eventually I decided he was right. His fingers curled tighter around mine, and I lost the total teacher sensei vibe he'd had a moment before. My skin tingled with his touch, and desire curled out from my belly, wrapping around my thighs and shooting up my spine.

Our eyes connected, and I felt dizzy at the emotion in his gaze. He kept everything locked away so tightly from everyone else. Just not from me.

"Never from you," he whispered, and I startled, jerking my hand back in confusion. Had he answered my thoughts? "You need your rest, Carlyle," he said, turning back to his laptop as though nothing weird at all had happened.

I could have gone back to my room, but something about the soft tapping of his fingers across the keyboard relaxed me and pulled my eyelids closed. Before I could summon the will to stand, I'd drifted to sleep right there on the couch.

CHAPTER TWENTY-SEVEN

CARLYLE

The next morning, I was sipping my second mug of super-sweet coffee when Jai shuffled into the kitchen, his expression like death.

"I thought you slept all day," I remarked as he gulped a glass of water from the tap. He slid his eyes to me and filled the glass again. "Do you need fresh blood or something?"

It was supposed to be a joke, but he looked ill as he processed the words.

"I do not partake in that filth," he said, his voice hoarse from sleep. "And I'm only awake now because my program finished running the data and came back with coordinates a few minutes ago. Where are the others?"

I shrugged. I'd been up about an hour, but I hadn't heard any signs of movement around the house. It was such a huge house that I could never tell where anyone was, or even if I was alone.

Jai slipped a cell phone from his sweatpants pocket. Even just rolled out of bed and grumpy, he still looked stylish, in a rumpled, indie rock sort of way. His slim-cut pants had a thick band at the bottom, and he wore woven sandals. His t-shirt looked soft enough to steal, and when he turned away, I finally saw how long his hair was.

Silky black layers reached to his mid-back, hanging in gentle, effortless waves - the kind of hair a girl would kill for. I'd never been much of a long-hair-on-guys type of girl, but hot damn, it was a sexy look on him.

After tapping out several texts, he tossed the phone on the counter and stretched his arms above his head. His shirt rode up enough for me to glimpse those delicious V shapes that cut guys have, and I had to force myself not to stare openly as he bundled his hair like a pro.

"They'll all be back in a bit."

I nodded, imagining him bundling my hair up like that and nipping my neck. Crap. I was at it again. So far, I'd fantasized about every single guy on the team except Toro, and I hadn't met him yet, so there was still time.

I made a sort of strangled groan, and Jai gave me a strange look. Again, I fought off the odd feeling that he knew what I was thinking.

"So you just eat normal food?" I asked, trying to fill the silence. He'd eaten pasta and bread with us, after all.

He leaned his hip against the counter and watched me for a long moment. "Many of my race do drink blood, like the humans put in their television. In Haret, I would have no issue participating, but it's different there. There should be no violence in the act. No taking of life."

"So, it's voluntary?" I clarified. He nodded. "Who volunteers?"

"Anyone may, but it is supposed to be a highly personal act - extremely sensual. It is most often done between lovers, which we call aima."

"Ah." There went my imagination. "Is that why you don't do it here? Because you don't have a, ah, partner?"

He pursed his lips. "I have never taken an aima."

This simple statement spawned a hundred questions, which I didn't get to ask, because Killian and Sol entered the room then, followed barely a minute later by Dair.

Jai gestured for us to all take a seat around the large table. He surveyed us like a proud papa - or at least a satisfied boss man. I grinned at him, and he allowed me a slip of a smile back before playing it straight again.

"Gentlemen, we seem to be on a winning streak. Thanks to the tracker Killian put on Jack, we were able to find a general location for one of the Underbelly camps. Along with Dair's locator spell, we now have very precise coordinates to check."

"Fuck yes!" Killian crowed, giving Sol a high five. Dair was smiling like the cat that got the canary.

Jai said, "We'll begin detail planning today, then begin extraction within thirty-six hours. The circus moves too fast for us to wait longer." He paused and served each of us a measured glance. "And although I wish we had much more time to prepare, I also think Carlyle should be involved in this mission."

Everyone went silent.

"Fuck yes!" I yelled, echoing Killian and earning a glare

from him. I didn't care - I was excited. I wanted this. It felt amazing to know Jai thought I could handle myself out there. I was part of the team, dammit.

I wasn't crying. Nope, not at all. That was just my eyes watering because the coffee was so fucking hot.

"Um, shortcake?" Sol said, breaking into my thoughts. "Out loud again."

"Shit," I muttered, casting my eyes down as someone chuckled. Jai reached over and squeezed my hand, surprising the hell out of me.

"Are you sure it's the best idea, taking her straight into Underbelly?" Sol said, his voice hesitant as he questioned Jai.

Jai frowned. "We're down two men. If one of us stays here to guard her, I'm afraid we wouldn't have enough bodies to infiltrate the camp."

"I don't need a babysitter," I said, huffing. Although I shouldn't have been protesting - I certainly didn't want Jai to change his mind.

"More than a few teams have fallen to the Ringmaster, if rumors are correct," Jai said. "I'm not taking any chances that this could be a trap. Certainly, he knows Jack made contact with us, so he'll be expecting us to turn up. I'd rather have you where we can see you and protect you than spend the whole mission worrying about you alone at the house."

I gave a thumbs up. It made sense - a little like LuAnn's philosophy of staying close on Underbelly's heels, so we'd always know where the threat was. Sol grumbled his agreement, and Jai nodded, settling the matter.

He straightened and said, "Okay team, this is it. Fuck this one up, and we may not get another chance before it's too late."

I couldn't help the snort that popped out, and Jai cut his eyes to me. "Great pep talk, boss." I smiled sweetly, and the corner of his lip twitched.

"Fuckin' hell, kid," Killian muttered.

Jai ignored us both and continued. "The location is about sixteen hours south by car, so we'll use Dair to transport. I've used satellites to survey the area and plot a bare map. I want Carlyle with Dair - the Ringmaster will certainly have magical security."

Sol grumbled something, but Jai shut him down with a single glance.

"Dair and Carlyle will take the western flank - stealth mode. There will almost certainly be magical barriers to break. Siphon in as far as you can. Practice that today," he added, and Dair nodded. "Use your locator spells to find Jack, then make a path out. Sol and Killian - beast mode on the opposite side. Create a distraction, so the extra security is drawn away from Dair. Mobilize anyone you find, but I want to minimize killing."

"Aw, man," Sol groaned, and Killian laughed.

Jai glared, silencing them. "Many of those people are not in the circus by choice. I don't want the blood of Haretian civilians on our hands."

Sol and Killian nodded, keeping their eyes down, and I watched them curiously. All this time, I'd never really thought about my guys as a military team. In my head, they'd been more like detectives.

"What are you going to be doing, boss?" I asked, wondering how Jai fit in. "Tech stuff?"

Jai rewarded me with the hint of a smile. "You just leave my part to me and your part to you," he said.

Everybody laughed, except me, because I had no idea what they were laughing at. I decided to let it go because I was included in the plan, and that was still awesome.

I looked at Dair. "Siphoning is that popping thing you do?" He nodded. "So once we get to the circus grounds, what do we do?"

"I'll cast a spell to keep our footsteps silent, and you'll cover me while I check the perimeter and perform another locator spell for Jack. You'll keep watch and tell me if anyone is coming - I'll need to conserve, and not needing to cast surveillance will help immensely." He smiled at me, and I felt all giddy and useful and stuff. "If you meet a human, you can use your power to put them to sleep, right?"

I nodded. "I helped LuAnn sleep plenty of times." I couldn't help but wonder what else I could do, though. Surely I could do more than follow Dair around like a puppy. I debated asking to channel someone's power, but it felt super awkward and the total opposite of the relationships I was trying to establish here.

I didn't want to be a party bus, so I didn't want any of them to feel like a charging plug.

"What about anyone who's from Haret?" I asked. There would probably be more of them than humans in an Underbelly camp.

"Leave any rogue Haretians to me," answered Dair, his navy eyes growing as cold as a moonless night. My heart started to beat twice as fast. Holy shit. I was about to go on a mission into the Underbelly - the one place I'd sworn never to end up. I was also going in with a bunch of killers. Good guys, but still.

This was actually happening.

"What about freeing any prisoners?" I asked, trying to swallow down my nerves.

Jai shook his head. "Our sole focus is Jack. I know that sounds cruel, but we need to focus on one task at a time. Assembling our team in full is our most important objective." He glared around the table at all of us. "This is an extraction-only mission. No getting sidetracked. Are we clear?"

I frowned, still not sold on his answer. Sol reached over and laced his fingers with mine.

"Once the Path is restored, we'll have all the power of Haret again, and the Ringmaster won't stand a chance. Anyone who's being held against their will can be set free then, I promise. We'll do it together, shortcake."

I nodded, pretending to be on board. It made sense, on one level, but I knew if I saw an opportunity to save a few kids, I'd sure as hell take it.

"Do not deviate from the plan, Carlyle," Jai warned again, looming over me. "Remember - we are highly trained, and we've been doing this for longer than you've been alive."

"I understand," I said, backing down. He was right. "I won't compromise you guys. Cross my heart and hope to die."

"What?" Killian barked out a laugh. "Why would you say that?"

I cocked my head at him. "You've never heard that? It's a promise."

"Sounds like a curse to me," he said.

"Well, curses aren't real," I said without thinking. The guys just blinked at me. "Ah. Curses are real, aren't they."

They all nodded, and I sighed. "Okay, we'll just go with

a spit shake."

Killian groaned. "Are we done for now, boss?"

"I'll call you back when the maps are ready. For now, prepare your equipment," Jai instructed.

"Make me a procurement list," Dair added. "Ready to practice siphoning?" he asked me, holding out a hand as he rose.

"As long as it doesn't hurt," I said. He laughed, and I groaned, smacking his hand away. "It's going to hurt. Goddamn it."

CHAPTER TWENTY-EIGHT

CARLYLE

Siphoning didn't hurt, as it turned out.

Instead, it made me vomit my guts up. Every. Motherfucking. Time.

Dair was sort of a sweetie, though, as he held my long hair back, shuffling his feet far enough away that I didn't spew on his expensive boots.

"I think that's enough," he said finally.

I coughed and wiped at my mouth, stumbling a little. All the loss of fluids had made me dizzy. I'd been drinking water between siphons, which helped a bit.

"It will get better, Cariño," he said, reaching to cup my cheek and brushing back a strand of my white-blond hair. I loved the soft roll of the word and how it was a play on both my name and the sweets I loved so much.

"When is that, again?" I muttered, but I was smiling. He chuckled.

"How about we practice some simple spells for a bit, instead? You won't have the magic yet, but you can learn the words and movements."

I nodded, noticing that he'd said yet. My stomach was already tumbling around again with the mere mention of channeling Dair's magic. He'd have to take a ride on the Carlyle party bus, and while my body was so ready, my mind was still resisting.

If I was being one hundred percent honest with myself, a big part of that rebellion was plain old fear that I wasn't quite sexy enough to live up to Dair's expectations.

He led me to a quiet part of the backyard, under a shady tree.

"*Parare stratum*," he said, twirling his fingers. A blanket appeared and spread itself on the grass. He repeated the spell several more times, procuring two plates, a partial box of donuts from breakfast, two mugs of coffee, a spoon, and the sugar bowl.

I eyed the donuts, but for once, I was more interested in what I was learning.

"So, '*parare*' must mean procure?" I asked, picking up on the common word in each demonstration. He nodded in appreciation. "How come I haven't heard you speak words with your little finger flicks before?"

"Advanced mages can learn to cast spells with intent, rather than spoken word. It's very difficult, and you must have extreme control over your mind. The 'finger flicks' can be avoided as well, but I prefer to let my brothers know when I'm performing a spell. It's also less draining."

"Okay, so, speak the words, flick the fingers. Sounds easy enough."

"You must also be fully focused on the intent of the spell. For example, I saw this particular blanket in the closet of my room earlier. I imagined its exact location and color, as well as the type of fabric and even the scent. I can't just ask the universe for a blanket and one appears from the cosmos. I'm simply moving items around, and I have to tell the magic exactly which object."

"Can you procure people?"

He frowned. "Living matter is entirely different, and animals of any type are much harder because they're in a constant state of motion - flux. Short answer, no, I can't. Long answer, it may be possible for someone of phenomenal power or decades of specific training."

"You can't procure something that's been moved, though? So if I'd gone in your room and moved all your shit around, you'd be helpless?" I snickered. That sounded like a mage prank waiting to happen.

Dair shrugged. "Yes, but I could just use a locator spell if I really needed something."

I nodded, beginning to see how the system worked. "Can you run out of magic?"

"Can you run out of energy?" he returned. "Everything has a limit, Carlyle. All power, all strength, all magic. All life - none of us is immortal, and none of us is infallible."

"Yes, sir," I mocked, but a bit of heat flashed in his eyes. Ah. So he liked to be boss, too. I filed that information away for the day I finally got the lady cajones to ask him to share his magic.

"Let's practice the motions first." He led me through a series of movements, and I giggled, feeling very much like a kid learning swish and flick all over again from the television. Then he procured a narrow leather book with phrases, written one to a page, with illustrations of the effect of each spell.

"Is this a kid's book?" I asked, flipping through the bright pages.

"A beginner's textbook. But yes, it's the one most often given to mages at age eight, when they begin training."

"Latin?" I guessed, and he nodded. "Why a human language?"

He grinned. "What makes you think it was human?"

Coughing away my surprise, I tried not to be so shocked. I shouldn't be surprised that Haretians had a hand in Earth's development, not when they lived such long lives here. I spoke a few of the phrases out loud, and he corrected my pronunciation. Over and over, I made the motions and said the words. It felt very silly, as I obviously was not going to make anything happen without channeling his magic.

It was pleasant spending time with Dair, though. He was a surprisingly patient teacher.

"Now, the final step is the intent. It's impossible for me to tell if you're doing that right, because you have no magic to test. Young mages are often taught to meditate first, so we can continue there."

"Ah, I'm great at that. Really," I insisted, when he slid me a look of skepticism. "LuAnn taught it to me. I used it whenever I was working in our booth, because pulling people's depression out of them is dangerous. If I pull all that negativity into myself, I could really be at risk of self-harm."

"So you meditated to do what, exactly?"

"To separate myself from the emotions I was pulling. To cordon them off in my brain, so that I could get rid of them or balance them."

He considered. "That should be sufficient to begin. When you work with intent, the idea is to quiet your mind of all stray thoughts. If I was trying to procure a blanket, but my mind was thinking about how thirsty I was, I might end up with a water bottle instead. Or, what often happens with young mages, is I'd procure both, but the bottle might be open and the blanket soaking wet."

"Got it. Don't think random thoughts." That would be a hard one for me. I glanced back to the bakery box on the blanket. "So can I have a donut now?"

He laughed and spread his palm as if to offer the food to me. I bit into a chocolate glazed donut, my eyes sliding closed in satisfaction.

Licking my fingers as I finished, I thought about the clothing he'd procured for me, presumably from a department store he'd visited before knowing I even existed. "You must just walk around and study everything. Do you have a photographic memory?"

His full lips twisted into a grin. "Something like that. I use spells to enhance my observation skills daily, and I practice more than a lot of mages. My skill and endurance are exceptionally high. Remember, each one of us was chosen for our expertise. Haret only sent the best to find the Qilin. That's another reason it's so important we find a way to return - there are so few of our echelon left." His voice was both determined and wistful, and I tried to imagine what it would be like to be separated from your home for so long.

I leaned forward and covered his hand with mine.

"We'll get Jack and Toro. And we'll find that damn Path. If I get to be a goddess, you guys get to be heroes."

His hand flipped beneath mine and squeezed back, and he leaned forward, meeting my gaze. "What more would you like to learn today?"

The question was simple, but the look in his eyes made it a challenge. Instead of answering with words, I gathered my courage. I'd gotten a bit of magic from Sol through a kiss - now I was ready for a taste of Dair's. Leaning forward, I pressed my lips briefly against his. He froze against me, and I drew back, hesitant. Maybe he didn't like the idea of me borrowing his magic?

Then he grasped the back of my neck, his fingers tangling in my loose hair, and drew me back in. His lips crashed over mine, his tongue parting my lips and thrusting into my mouth with long, forceful strokes. I felt the tingle of energy I'd noticed with Sol, and I wondered if that was the magic transferring to me.

I broke away, excited to try a spell. Dair laughed at me, his voice low and velvety.

"So impatient. When you're ready to truly take my magic, you'll need to learn a little more composure."

"You mean submission?" I guessed, wondering if I was right about his preferred flavor.

"Absolutely," he growled, reaching to grasp my hands. He guided my fingers through the motions once more, whispering the Latin along with me. "Now clear your mind and imagine what you want to move."

I focused on a tiny flower growing a few feet away. I didn't know the Latin for flower, or even the name of the deep purple blossom. I quieted everything else in my brain, slipping into the same blank-canvas mode I'd used to work festivals for years.

"*Parare*," I whispered, making the required motion with my fingers. My skin tingled, and I felt the tendrils of power I'd gained from Dair begin to gather in my fingertips.

The flower trembled as though caught in a breeze.

"*Parare*," I said again, this time imagining the magic as a sort of extension of my fingers, like tendrils reaching to pluck the stem. I laughed in shock as the flower floated through the air, landing neatly in my palm.

I brought it to my nose and inhaled, grinning over at a stunned Dair. "What? Didn't think I'd do it the first time?" I teased, nuzzling the velvety petals against my cheek.

He blinked. "It's a flower."

"Ah, no shit, Sherlock."

"Carlyle, it's a living organism. That's incredibly advanced." He'd sat up straight, and his eyes were gleaming. "You just performed a spell it took me several years to perform consistently. *And* you powered it with just a kiss."

His words hit home in a rush, and I sat back on my heels. Hell *yes* - I really was going to be a help to the team, not just dead weight. I grinned to myself. "Well, fuck me sideways," I whispered, glee zinging through my chest.

Dair sucked in a sharp breath, and I looked up at him. His grin had grown wolfish, and my cheeks heated as I realized what I'd just said. "Now, *that* would be an interesting experiment," he murmured.

I gulped. I was so not ready for that, but maybe... maybe something more than a kiss. I shook my head. I needed to work with what he'd already given me. We needed to see how much power I'd gotten from just a kiss.

Dair was not a charging cord, I reminded myself.

"Again," he prompted, gesturing to the blanket beneath us. "Try to move these objects around."

I repeated the spell several times, moving the donuts and coffee around the blanket. Then I walked around the corner of the house, where I couldn't see our picnic anymore, and tried it.

My magic began to fizzle at that point. I managed to drag the blanket a few feet, but not to actually procure it.

"Still impressive, I think," Dair assessed. "You may also get more range and endurance with practice."

I hummed in agreement, distracted by what I was thinking. I wanted more magic. I wanted more spells to use as weapons in my arsenal for this mission. Besides, if I was being fucking honest, I wanted more Dair.

"What is it?" he asked, and I realized I'd been glaring into the distance.

I took a deep breath. "I'm worried I won't be much help rescuing Jack. I don't want to let anyone down," I said, biting down on my bottom lip.

"Ah, Cariño. Don't be too hard on yourself. You've barely just found out what you are. You're coming on the mission to help us focus, not help us fight."

I sighed. "I want to help with everything, though." I looked up at him, holding his gaze long enough that he cocked his head in question. He knew, I thought. He knew what I wanted - I could see it in the tiny twist of his lips. He just wanted me to say it out loud.

He wanted me to ask for it.

"Can we… can we try a little bit more?" I rushed out. "I need more magic."

CHAPTER TWENTY-NINE

CARLYLE

Dair stared down at me, eyes liquid with lust.

"You want more?" he asked, his voice low and rough.

"Not... everything. But more," I whispered, my stomach fluttering like a first-timer. I did need his magic for this mission, I reasoned.

Even more than that, I thought I just might be ready to sample Dair's particular tastes. Maybe. I'd never been with a man who liked a side of pain with his pleasure, and I was fucking curious to see if I'd like it, too.

"I don't want you against a cement wall, grunting like an animal," he warned.

A snicker escaped my mouth, but I nodded in agreement. I fully expected candles and champagne to accompany this lesson.

"Will you play by my rules, then?" he asked, his words barely audible between us. "The first rule, of course, is you can always say no."

"And the second?" I asked, a little breathless beneath his gaze.

"The second rule is if you don't say no, you can only say yes."

I tilted my head, a little confused.

"Good girls wait to be told what to do," he murmured. "So, if you're a good girl, go to my bedroom and undress, then put on the clothes I'll provide."

"What if I'm a bad girl?" I asked, because I had to know the game to play it.

"Then the game is over."

I forced myself to nod, ignoring my nerves, and his smile grew feral.

He did his popping into thin air thing, and I headed into the house on shaky legs. I padded upstairs and down the hall to the closed door I knew was his. I expected him to be there, but he wasn't. Instead, the navy blue comforter and canopy bed already held four items - two sheer black stockings, a scrap of satin that might be panties, and a garter belt.

My heart hammered in my chest as I began to follow his instructions, sliding my shirt over my head.

Not knowing what to expect was driving me crazy. Dair loved drama and control - that much was evident in the clothes he chose. The silence in the room was oppressive, and my fingers trembled as I pulled down my leggings and lacy underwear.

Leaning against the bed, I tried to put on one of the

stockings, but my fingernail snagged it, and a run started up the side. Shit.

If he came back and I wasn't ready yet, he'd assume I'd changed my mind. I struggled harder with the stocking, only making the run worse.

Throwing the fabric on the bed, I scooped up the tiny triangle of satin, trying to make sense of the long, tangled strings.

Goddamn it, I sucked at this seduction stuff. I sat on the bed and tossed the panties away in frustration. I had no business with these fancy, stolen clothes. Apparently I had no business with a sophisticated, dominant man like Dair, either.

"Is there a problem?" Dair's voice surged into the room as he strode toward me, the door banging shut behind him.

I jumped to my feet, feeling the frustration boil over. "Why do you want-"

"No more words," Dair commanded, crowding me against the bed. "I want what I want, and you've agreed to give it to me like a good girl, now haven't you? Nod once for yes, or prepare to be punished."

Heat flared in his eyes as he stared down at my naked body, and I squirmed against the overpowering desire pooling in my core. Fuck me, I wanted him, despite my anxiety. I'd just never done anything like this.

"Carlyle," Dair prompted. I raised my eyes to meet his dark blue ones, and his gaze softened for just a moment. "You're always able to say no," he whispered.

As soon as the option was on the table, I didn't want it anymore - didn't need it. I no longer felt trapped or controlled, and I found myself nodding in certainty.

Dair's lips curled up, and he snatched both of my wrists together in one hand before I could move. Stretching my arms above my head, he forced me to stand. Then he reached up and pulled down a loop from the canopy frame - a leather strap I hadn't noticed before.

Staring deep into my eyes, Dair threaded my hands through the loop and tightened a buckle. I didn't resist, and if I were being honest, I didn't want to resist. My body was naked and stretched tall before him, and every fucking nerve was sparking with anticipation.

"Good girls do as they're told, and I told you to get dressed," Dair said coldly. "Now, I'll have to dress you myself."

His fingers trailed from my hands, down my arms, to my heaving rib cage. The musky scent of tobacco wove around me. He lingered on the fullness of my breasts, but he never once touched the aching peaks of my nipples. I made a noise of protest as his hands traveled toward my waist, and suddenly, his grip tightened painfully on my hip.

The crisp bite of his champagne scent slid across my skin.

"Good girls wait," he growled, his lips hot against my neck. I moaned softly as he trailed his tongue lightly down my throat, his fingers now massaging the hip they'd been clutching. Dair dropped to one knee before me and lifted one of my feet, then the other, as he pulled the satin panties up, stopping at my thighs.

I felt like I was going to go plum crazy with desire, and he'd barely touched me. He was putting *on* my clothes, for fuck's sake.

Dair chuckled as though he could read my mind, and tugged the panties up a few more inches. He paused to tighten the strings, and they cut into my skin, a thin pinch across my ass. I gasped as he smoothed away that brief pain, then pulled the panties all the way up and tied the ends into perfect bows.

The black silk fit perfectly against my skin, and I whimpered a little as Dair repeated the torturous work again with each sheer black stocking, then cinched the garter belt around my waist.

He bent lower to fasten the garters to the stockings, kissing and licking along the lacy edge of each stocking until he reached the velvety skin at the top of my thigh.

My sex clenched as he came so close, but never fucking close enough. "Please," I whispered, before I could help myself.

The crack of his palm on my ass was so sudden that I cried out, but my voice dropped into a dizzy hum as Dair pressed his tongue flat against the silk covering my pussy.

Heat teased my opening without hope as he refused to move or lick. I writhed against his tongue, needing so much more, but he only clamped his fingers around my hips. Removing his tongue and leaning back to look up at me, he smirked. God, I wished I could knot my fingers in his dark curls and press his mouth to my center.

"Good girls wait," he reminded me. "And good girls get to cum."

I struggled a moment against the strangeness of his dominance and my submission. I wanted him, and I was getting fucking impatient.

"Do you want to cum, Cariño?" he asked, and I nodded, frustration spilling over into a light sigh. "Then be good, because waiting makes it better."

I knew I could free my hands at any moment. The loop

was tight, but not a trap. His fingers were hard on my skin, but they would give way the second I asked. By now, I really, really wanted the release he was offering.

So I nodded, letting my body go pliant beneath his grip.

Humming in satisfaction, Dair nudged my legs apart a few more inches. The movement made me shorter, and the leather on my wrists grew tighter. Feathering his fingers along the edges of the garters, up and down over the curve of my ass, Dair leaned in and blew his warm breath over my already-soaked panties.

I bit down on a moan. It was so goddamn hard to be good.

His tongue pressed hard against the crotch of the panties again, and this time he licked lazily at my clit through the fabric coating it. His fingers wandered down the string of the thong, spreading my ass gently as he continued to tease my clit through the silk.

I bucked against his face, feeling a little insane with the lack of more. He clicked his tongue at me, and the second I grew still again, he pulled the panties to the side and sunk two long fingers into my soaked pussy, his tongue finally swirling around my bare clit. I cried out as he brought me nearly to the edge within seconds, only to withdraw his tongue.

He pumped his fingers inside me, faster and faster, hooking them to find that most delicious spot.

I panted with the effort of trying to stay still, waves of tremors shaking my thighs, and finally, he clamped his lips around my clit and sucked it hard. He stretched me with a third finger and fucked me ferociously until I shattered above him with a scream.

My knees grew weak enough that I was effectively

hanging by my wrists, and Dair shifted his shoulders between my legs to support me. His motions slowed, but he still pumped and sucked without mercy as the aftershocks of orgasm rippled through my body, and I moaned his name.

When he finally withdrew his fingers, my head lolled back, and I felt drunk on pleasure. *Masterful,* was the word floating in my mind.

Dair reached up and unbuckled my wrists, leaning me gently back on the bed. He climbed over me, sliding up my naked body and reawakening all those quivering nerves. He kissed me hard, my taste mingling on our tongues as his wet fingers kneaded my breast.

I felt a second orgasm building as he rolled my nipple and kissed me with powerful, slow strokes of his tongue.

His cock pressed hard between my spread legs, straining against his dress pants. When I began to reach for it, though, he grabbed my wrists above my head again, locking them together in one of his big hands. He ground against me, the soaking silk of my panties stuttering across the smooth fabric of his slacks.

"Come for me again, Cariño," he murmured. He reached down and pressed a thumb against my swollen clit, then slipped his fingers inside me again. I cried out as pleasure ripped through me. My legs shook as I pressed them against his body, caging him in, too.

He kissed me one last time, trailing his wet fingers up my naked skin. Then he raised himself and looked down at me in satisfaction.

"You were a very good girl," he said, his smile hooking up on one side in complete satisfaction. "Although your new panties are completely ruined. We will have to-"

A knock at the door interrupted whatever he had planned next. "What?" Dair barked out, adjusting his slacks over an impressive bulge.

"Did Carlyle come up here?" It was Killian.

I smothered a giggle - I sure fucking had. Twice.

"Shall we see if our little experiment worked?" Dair said, his voice low as he handed me a white satin robe. I blinked at it. Where had... ah. He must have just procured it.

Whatever. I was past caring.

I tied the robe shut and nodded. Dair flicked his fingers, and the door opened. Killian took in the scene in a split second, then glared at Dair, his lip curling up in disgust.

"Carlyle has been learning magic," Dair said, his voice lilting with challenge.

"I fuckin' bet," Killian muttered.

"Show him, Cariño," Dair whispered. "Just as we practiced - twist of the wrist and flick of the fingers and..."

I closed my eyes, repeated the movement and words, and asked the power to come.

"Fuck!" Killian yelled as soft fabric hit me in the face. I opened my eyes and broke into laughter. Balled in my hands was Killian's shirt, and he was standing before us, bare-chested and open-mouthed.

It was actually a very good look on him. I smirked, but before I could try to procure anything else, Killian stalked into the room and snatched back his shirt.

"Keep playing your games, little girl. But I donna think ye are ready for me to play back."

He sauntered from the room, and I ogled the mass of

tattoos spreading across his back.

I'd need longer than a few seconds to study that canvas. Maybe there were even more, hiding under those low-slung jeans. I bit down on another grin, even knowing my face had flushed bright red.

CHAPTER THIRTY

CARLYLE

I spent the rest of the evening lounging on the couch, memorizing spells and practicing hand movements.

I'd decided not to use any magic until the next morning before the mission, to see how long the channeling might last. Dair's bedroom antics were definitely worth repeating, but I couldn't be running off to do dirty things every time I needed to cast a spell or lift something heavy.

Surely, I could figure out how to make the power stick around longer.

The guys all left me alone, caught up in their responsibilities and preparations for the mission. Killian never even came back to find me, so I wasn't sure what he'd wanted. I was kind of okay with having a night off from his snark, because my nerves were buzzing as I thought about the next day.

I wanted to help the team, but I was so nervous that I would screw up, that the Ringmaster would get me, or that one of the guys would get hurt.

I was questioning everything, although my instinct still told me I was in the right place. I'd always gone by my gut, and my gut told me these were my guys - I needed to be wherever they were.

By the time my eyes were heavy with the need to sleep, my brain was too revved up for it again.

"You should get to sleep, shortcake," Sol said as he came into the living room. His shirt was soaked through with sweat. "Being tired on a mission is the worst," he added, his tone a warning.

I stood, stretching my arms high over my head and yawning. "I'm not sure I'll be able to sleep," I admitted.

"It's okay to be nervous. Dair will take good care of you, and the rest of us won't be far." He reached a large hand out and palmed the back of my head, sliding his fingers through my hair. I shivered a tiny bit at the touch, and when his hand dropped back to his side, my body felt the loss immediately.

I wanted to ask if I could snuggle next to him tonight, but I wasn't sure if he wanted me for something like that. He'd told Dair fucking and claiming were the same, but in my heart I knew they were different - to both of us. I just wasn't sure if he was ready to do boyfriend things like snuggle.

I also wasn't sure if I was ready to admit I wanted him to do boyfriend things.

I cast my eyes down, fiddling with my beginner's spell

book.

"Hey," Sol murmured, hooking a finger under my chin. "Let me grab a quick shower, and I'll come rub your feet or something until you can fall asleep."

I couldn't help the huge smile that broke over my face, and he startled, then answered me with a happy grin of his own. Before he could change his mind or say anything else, I scampered out of the room and up the stairs to my room. I slipped into a pair of loose shorts and a tank.

Eying my cold bed, though, I decided not to get in it. Instead, I crept down the hall to Sol's room.

The water was still running in his attached bathroom as I slipped into his bed, grinning like mad at the idea of catching him off guard. I pulled the covers up to my eyeballs and turned my face toward the bathroom door.

He did not disappoint. I watched a little breathlessly as the big man toed open the door, scrubbing at his hair with the towel I'd expected to be wrapped around his waist. I swallowed hard.

Fuck, his body was beautiful - all that golden skin wrapping muscle after rippling muscle. Like my own little hero action figure, come to life to play.

Okay, so Sol naked and wet with cooling water droplets and me in his bed might not be conducive to sleep.

I was totally on board with that.

"Fuck!" he shouted as his eyes finally snagged on my form in his bed. The noise turned quickly to a predatory growl as I didn't blink away from his body, silhouetted in the steam behind him. He dropped the towel completely and slunk toward the bed, totally comfortable in his nakedness.

His cock hardened as he walked, rising to full attention

as he lay down on his side on top of the covers, pinning me beneath them.

"Shortcake," he murmured, burying his face in my hair and resting a heavy arm across my middle. "This isn't what I was implying, just so you know."

I wiggled my shoulders free and propped up on my elbow to look him in the eyes. "Me neither, to be honest." I grabbed his hand and took a deep breath. A slice of fear shot through my chest as I realized his smell was a little different.

The sexy summer afternoon scent was there, but it was laced through with a bit of autumn chill. Hesitancy.

I sat up farther, barely touching him.

Maybe he didn't want me in his room - maybe I'd crossed an invisible line and made him uncomfortable. His body was still saying yes, but his heart was saying maybe not.

"What is it?" I whispered, crossing my arms over my chest and slumping down.

Sol tugged his fingers through his damp, tousled hair, his face pained. "I just don't ever want you to feel forced. Or obligated."

I shook my head - I didn't. Maybe he did, though? I never wanted to do that to anyone.

"The way your power works - I know you're nervous about tomorrow. I'll gladly give you a shot of strength to keep you safe, but we can keep you safe without it, too. Your body is yours for pleasure. Not ours for power."

I swear, my jaw dropped, just like they always say in the books. I stared at him for an embarrassing amount of time before his words totally filtered into my brain.

I honestly hadn't thought of myself like that at all, but

now that he'd pointed it out to me, it was all I could think about.

Oh, god.

"What if the Ringmaster knows about my power and he... and he wants..." I couldn't finish speaking the horrible thought that had dropped onto my brain like a nuclear bomb.

The wrong people could make me into a formidable weapon - forcing themselves on me and their power into me.

"Hey - no. Don't," Sol soothed, sitting up to wrap me in his arms, blanket and all. His steady warmth contrasted the chill that had swept over my skin, making me realize how badly I was shaking. "Listen to me, shortcake. For one, the Ringmaster will never get his hands on you. *Never.* And for two, I don't think Qilin power works like that. I don't know for sure, but I think you have to, ah, enjoy yourself?"

His awkward ending jerked me back from my fear free fall, startling a snort from me. I buried my face in his neck, nuzzling into his warmth like a kitten. His arms tightened around me.

"Carlyle," he whispered, but it was more like a prayer than the beginning of a request.

The desire in me settled into something more liquid and warm, like the relief of sinking into a warm bath. I felt safe and protected - with an entirely new edge to it that my touch-drunk heart labeled "loved." My sensible brain scoffed, though. Who was I to even identify love, much less have earned it from someone in a few short days?

I pushed my hair from my face and smiled up at him. "So, maybe I could get that foot rub now?"

He smiled and stood up, turning his tight ass toward me as he grabbed a pair of shorts from a drawer. I smirked as I noted the lack of underwear - I loved commando at night, too. It was just more comfy.

"You're okay to sleep in here, if you want," he said, his voice uncertain. That warm-bath feeling grew, squeezing my heart a little. My throat closed up suspiciously, and all I could manage was a nod as I scooted toward the middle of the bed to make more room.

He sat across the far end, lifting the covers to find my bare feet. I closed my eyes and sighed as his strong fingers kneaded away the stress I was feeling about the coming day, and I dropped so fast into sleep that I didn't even remember him joining me under the blanket.

CHAPTER THIRTY-ONE

CARLYLE

I woke to a shaft of sunlight streaming in from the open curtains. Stretching and arching my back, I found another shaft - Sol was pressed against me from behind, a low, rumbling sort of purr emanating from his bare chest.

"Morning, shortcake," he whispered, then lowered his mouth to my shoulder. I shivered at the feather-light touch, and my body jolted awake.

Sol pressed another kiss at the neckline of my tank top, and I stretched my neck in invitation. The tip of his tongue licked a fiery trail over my pulse point, flicking over my collarbone, then up toward my jaw. I turned my face just enough to meet his lips, and he made a satisfied sort of rumble as he delved into my mouth.

His tongue tangled with mine in long, powerful strokes - there were no teasing nips this morning as he pressed my head deep into the pillow.

One hand slid beneath my neck, fisting my hair and keeping me open and close for his kisses, but the other began to wander. Lower and lower, he walked his fingers on a torturous path. Kneading gently around the side of my breast, then sliding along the middle of my ribcage, then toying with the edge of my shorts.

"Are you sure?" he rasped, but I only kissed him harder, arching my back against his front and rubbing myself against his cock. He growled, and his fingers slipped beneath my shorts. I felt his lips grin against mine as he found out I wasn't wearing panties. Cupping my bare pussy in his large palm, he slowed his kisses to a much lazier pace.

I wiggled against his hand, growing impatient, and he chuckled, but his fingers spread, going deeper between my thighs. One finger slid through my folds, while his thumb circled my aching clit. Way too gently, he slipped a finger into my heat, and I moaned, thrusting my hips a little in hopes he would start some friction.

"You're so hot for it," he said, his voice strained. I grinned and wiggled my ass against his cock again. I'd felt shame with boys before - how my desire seemed so much more intense than theirs. Meeting Sol and the others had woken my true nature even more, but I felt nothing but power as I encouraged him.

He pinned my back tight to his front, his palm locked against my pussy, and he kissed and sucked his way down my neck as his finger began to twist and pump into me.

I moaned and arched into the sensation, and he began

to thrust his hips into my ass, grinding against me through his shorts. His breath hitched against my skin in little puffs. He added a second finger, circling my clit as he ramped me higher.

Latching his lips onto my neck, he sucked hard and increased the speed of both his hips and his fingers. When his thumb finally pressed into my throbbing clit, I shattered, shaking against his iron grip as my body rippled with pleasure.

Panting, I rode his fingers, prolonging my pleasure as much as possible.

Finally coming down from my high, I twisted in his grasp, intent on repaying the feeling. I slithered down his chest, licking and kissing my way over each ripple. I kicked the covers off us as I yanked down his athletic shorts and freed his cock.

"Get it," he whispered, his eyes heavy-lidded as he watched. His arms were stretched above his head, his muscles bunching. I grasped his thick shaft in my fingers and slid them up and down, slow and teasing. My tongue licked down that gorgeous Adonis belt, and his breath hitched.

I teased his head, the tip silky against my lips. He groaned, and I smirked before plunging my mouth down on his cock, taking him deep into my throat.

Sol gave a strained shout, his muscles tightening beneath me. I worked my mouth up and down, twirling my fingers around his base.

He'd just begun to pant a bit when the door burst open. My eyes flew up, and my surprised glare met Killian's fiery golden gaze. His hair was sleep-mussed, and he held a knife before him, ready to strike.

"Ah, fuckin' hell, kid," he yelled, slamming a fist into the door jam. He fixed his eyes on the opposite wall, refusing to look at where I was straddling Sol's thighs, his cock heavy between my lips. "I heard you yell, and I thought you were bein' fuckin' attacked."

Sol chuckled, his hand wandering down to my hair. Gently, he pressed my mouth down his cock again, encouraging me to continue. His hips lifted in a half-thrust, filling my throat.

"Quit acting jealous, Kills," he managed, his voice thick with desire. I wasn't sure what game he was playing, but I was enjoying the idea of Killian being jealous. It wasn't true, of course, but I wouldn't mind a taste of the redhead one day.

Two days ago, I'd been operating under different rules - don't feed the sex addiction.

Now I knew my desire made me powerful instead of the opposite.

I moaned around Sol's cock, sucking harder and moving faster. My eyes slid closed, but somehow I knew Killian had turned his gaze back to me. He was watching, and it was *hot*.

"Gah! It's turned into a fuckin' bordello around here," Killian ground out from behind us, and I heard the door slam.

Part of me wanted to stop and run after him - confront him on his shitty attitude. Sol's fingers tightened in my hair, though, and I could feel his cock swell against my tongue. I pushed away my anger with Killian and took Sol even deeper, squeezing his shaft and cupping my hand around his tightening balls.

With a roar, he came in my mouth, spilling hot cum

down my throat. I swallowed it all, feeling greedy and satisfied. I licked up his shaft one last time as I sat back on my heels, grinning at Sol. His muscles twitched as he threw his forearm over his eyes.

"Fuck," he breathed. "Never in my life… "

I giggled. "That good, huh?" I teased. "You make it easy."

His mouth stretched into a grin beneath his arm. "I'm keeping you, shortcake. Anything you want - just tell your lion."

Right now, I wanted about three mugs of coffee and a dozen pastries. I figured that was already waiting for me in the kitchen, though. Stretching my legs down to the floor, I couldn't help but start to think about the day to come and the mission to get Jack.

"I want to keep you, too," I whispered, half to myself as I rested a hand on the doorknob. And by "you," I meant all of them.

Sol hauled himself to a sitting position, adjusting his shorts back to his waist. "Hey, don't worry about Kills," he said, misinterpreting me. "Carlyle," he prompted, and I turned back to look at him. "He'll come around. There's a lot going on in that fae head of his, and losing Jack and Toro just as we found you is killing him. He's all turned around. But wanna know a secret?" He grinned conspiratorially.

I nodded, a smile slipping onto my face. He was so cute, with his sexy tangle of hair.

"He *likes* to watch."

A shiver shot up my spine as Sol's words confirmed the sense I'd had earlier. I still doubted Killian had any real desire for me - too bad I was already lost again, imagining the different ways his "fuck and suck" might work.

Feeling my fingernails dig into my skin, I gasped as I realized my grip on the doorknob was way too tight. I'd crushed the smooth metal knob beneath my fingers.

Sol snickered as he saw it, too, and I flew out of the room, heat flaming across my cheeks.

Now we both knew I wanted Killian, but I'd never admit it to the arrogant fae. I was just a kid sister with a crush to him.

CHAPTER THIRTY-TWO

CARLYLE

The day passed in a whirlwind of last-minute tips on spells from Dair and defensive moves from Sol, although I doubted I'd remember half of it if I was attacked.

Jai briefed everyone on the latest scans from his drone, showing us map after map of what we might find. I barely understood a word, though I tried hard to hide my confusion and frustration. None of his intel was complete. We were flying blind in too many ways, but I truly trusted my guys to keep me safe.

The main problem was Underbelly's protective magic was too strong for Jai's human tech, and Killian and Dair both admitted the protective spells were too complex for either of them to unravel all its secrets. It was a crazy-ass mission, but none of us had any thoughts of backing down.

I knew it had only been a few days since I'd been so mad at Jack I could have killed him myself, but learning to care for his team and seeing their determination to bring him home had changed my mind. These were my guys, and I felt the need to complete our group almost as strongly as they did.

As long as I didn't think too hard about it, I didn't get freaked out by the intensity of my feelings for this pack I was secretly starting to think of as family.

After a quick, late dinner of frozen pizza, we dressed in SWAT-style outfits, decking out in solid black, dozens of weapons, and little spy ear-pieces so we could communicate with each other. Dair had wanted to siphon somewhere to get special sizes for me, but Jai had ruled it a waste of his magic. I had to agree - my gear was less fancy, but just as useful. I had my shit-kicker boots, an adapted bullet-proof vest, and a cut-down belt of knives.

"Don't be too reliant on any of this," Jai warned as I slipped a handful of knives into their sheaths. "There are too many Haretian powers that make these human weapons pointless, and human tech is often overpowered by glamor or other spells."

"Yeh, kiddo," Killian mocked as he strutted by, snagging one of the knives without even touching me. "I can make my air pull that metal right off your body - plenty o' others can, too."

I snatched it back from his hand, glaring. "It won't hurt to be prepared. As you've seen, I've had a taste of strength and spells, too," I added, narrowing my eyes at him as I spoke. He scowled and sauntered out of the room, flipping me off as he left.

Sol chuckled from the other side of the table. "Get it, shortcake," he muttered, echoing what he'd said to me just before I'd taken him deep in my throat, and I flushed.

"It's time," Jai interrupted. It was just past midnight. Dair nodded, grabbed Sol by the shoulder, and popped out of the house in an instant. Mere minutes had passed before he returned and did the same with Killian, then Jai.

Alone in the house, I tapped my foot rapidly against the floor as I waited for my turn. The air squeezed around my ears, and Dair was in front of me again.

"Ready?" he asked.

"Sure," I lied. I took a deep breath. "Let's go fuck some shit up."

He laughed and bent to me, pressing his lips against mine. His mouth moved against mine as he spoke, and I shivered, wishing we had time for just a little more. "Don't do a single dangerous thing, Cariño. Jai wouldn't put you in there without believing you can take it, but I'm just not ready to give you up. There are still so many things to teach you about being a good girl."

He thrust his tongue into my mouth, pushing my head back with the force of his kiss and plunging deep enough to rock my core. Palming my ass through my tight black pants, he sucked me into the siphon.

All I could think was the man was a damn liar. He'd promised siphoning would get better, but the gut-wrenching sensation wasn't a bit more bearable.

My stomach felt like it was being sucked through my throat and shoved back down again, and my brain was being squashed against my skull. My arms and legs shook like jelly.

Dropping onto the still-warm summer grass of an empty, dark hay field, I dry-heaved, cursing Dair's magic with every gag. No car for us - nope. Had to fucking siphon in.

"This is it?" I asked, hauling myself up. The night was lit with a full moon, and in the distance, I could barely make out a line of short trailers and a few scattered pickup trucks. It seemed very empty and plain, and there was nothing visible in the way of security.

"Maybe this part isn't the main camp," Dair suggested. "Jai wasn't certain how far out we'd arrive. Let's just stick to the plan and check the perimeter."

He strode off toward what I assumed was east, and I followed, noticing my footsteps were spelled silent as promised. As we approached the first pickup truck, the hairs on the back of my neck began to raise, and my skin tingled as though someone were watching me.

Dair held up two fingers in our signal to stop. "I can sense magic. Can you feel it?" he whispered.

I nodded, realizing that must be the prickly feeling across my skin. It was a little like when Dair had shown me how to do spells. He waved his hand and recited a spell I hadn't heard before, and a soft, silvery glow spread through the air before us, collecting across an invisible wall like steam clinging to a mirror.

"Barrier," he whispered, repeating the same into his ear-piece. He nodded, just as I heard Killian's voice in my ear confirming they had found the same on their side.

I stretched out my hand until it pressed against an invisible solid, like a glass wall. There was no temperature or texture to it, but I couldn't press through, no matter how hard I pushed.

We walked along the edge of the barrier for several minutes, Dair spreading his spell so we would see if there was a gap.

"Can you break through it?" I asked. Everything was too quiet for my liking - I'd seen too many festivals to believe all the freaks were fast asleep already.

He shrugged. "Possibly. It's not very thick. That amount of magic would just attract a lot of attention." We kept to the edge, as much in the shadows as possible.

"Where are all the people?" I whispered, getting more and more creeped out. It was like a ghost town.

As if I'd summoned them with my question, two muscled men stepped out from behind a nearby trailer, fixing us in their hard stares. Dair cut his eyes to me and glanced pointedly at the lack of his magical glow - there was a break in the barrier here. My stomach tightened in anticipation of a fight.

"Identify," one of the men said, leveling a silver pistol at us.

Dair glanced at me, his eyes warning me to stay quiet. "We heard there was a circus around here. Thought we might join up," he said.

Pistol Guy snorted. "Dressed like Mission Impossible? Don't think so."

The second guy cracked his knuckles, flexing his huge arms in the most dumbass stereotype ever. I breathed in deep, nearly gagging on the dank rust scent of their human cockiness. A grin crept onto my face, and Pistol Guy swung his glare to me. The air shifted a bit, and I grimaced at the warm beer scent of his lust. Gross.

I stepped a bit closer to Dair, who gave the men a charming smile and said, "My friend and I are simply searching for a new place to practice our special skills."

I bit down on a laugh, waiting for my signal.

"Shall we, Cariño?" he said, and I knew it was time. Dair rattled off a simple procurement spell, and Pistol Guy lost his defining feature with a shout of surprise. Dair tackled him instantly, flinging both fists and spells.

I darted behind the behemoth and stretched high to wrap my fingers around the base of his neck. Shoving a bone-weary fatigue into him as hard as I could, I relished the rush of power leaving my body. He dropped to his face in the dirt, and I rode him right down to the ground. Stepping away gracefully, I had just enough time to see Dair crack the other guy's temple with the butt of the gun.

"Very good," Dair said, fashioning magical handcuffs for each man. "First in," he gloated into the earpiece, and I grinned at a good-natured curse from Sol. Dair crowded me against the trailer and kissed me hard and fast, and I decided I liked winning. I felt a zing of magic top me off as he pulled me through the slit in the barrier.

Now we were in the center section, where Jai's drones had zeroed out and produced little more than fuzzy, shifting images. Part of me knew our entry had been way too easy, though.

CHAPTER THIRTY-THREE

CARLYLE

"Can you sense Jack anywhere?" I asked Dair as we crept through the lines of dark trailers. I was still suspicious of why everything was so quiet, and I thought Dair was growing more nervous, too. Underbelly wasn't living up to its reputation, and I was starting to feel like a mouse being lured right into the snake's gaping mouth.

"I'm not certain." Dair sounded mildly offended, as though he'd never come across such a thing as uncertainty. "It feels like he's been here, but I can't say for sure if he's *still* here. It's maddening, actually, like those fun-house mirrors that reflect so many times you can't tell where anything is."

Jai's voice slipped into my ear, low and melodious. "I'm

in. There are tents set up, but I can't get near enough to see anything - too many guards to risk. I can hear them practicing a lion tamer act."

Sol growled across the airwaves, his anger vibrating my ear. My heart constricted, thinking of how much crueler a circus animal act could be if the animals were actually shifters.

I saw the tightening in Dair's jaw, too, and it ramped up my anxiety. I didn't have much to compare the guys to, but they'd seemed pretty damn powerful up until now. If they were nervous, I was terrified.

"Do you think we could get someone to tell us any information? Or should we just keep sneaking around?" I asked.

"We need to stay off the radar - take our cues from Jai," he answered, his voice more sure. I nodded, following him as he stepped silently between the darkened trailers. Up ahead, we finally glimpsed life as a group of people gathered around a portable fire pit. We drew in as close as possible without giving ourselves away. Dair whispered another spell, and suddenly I could hear the people's words much better. A few girls were laughing as a pair of boys took turns singing rounds of a dirty song. Several were playing cards, and others were passing a bottle around.

We listened for several seconds, but we didn't hear anything about anyone named Jack or a dragon shifter or even the Ringmaster himself. Watching the young people laugh and joke, I began to wonder if Underbelly Circus was really as horrible as everyone had told me.

Surely there was more to it than this.

"Are these people human?" Dair asked me, arching an

eyebrow to let me know I was being tested. I breathed deeply, carefully separating smoke and ash, gasoline, and the rusted metal scent of the trailers all around us. Gradually, I began to pick out individual scents that were definitely human.

I nodded, though I could still sense traces of magic. There must be a few Haretians mixed in the group, or else the area was spelled with something. "What do you want me to do with them?"

"Nothing." Dair's voice was troubled, though he didn't offer an explanation.

We listened a few more minutes but heard nothing of value, so we skirted the area and moved deeper into the circus camp.

According to Jai's drone scans, the trailers formed a giant semi-circle. He'd been unable to see anything at all in the center, and now that we were here, neither could we.

An empty field stretched before us, just where the main circus camp should be. Frustrated, I shoved past Dair and waded into the thick grass, hoping any snakes would scatter. Dair reached for my arm, but I jerked away, only to run smack into a new barrier.

"Fuck," I groaned, rubbing the point of my nose.

Dair looked grim as he sent out his magic to show me where the barrier was. It felt like more than just a magical barrier, though - thicker somehow. Like the difference between water and honey. I looked to Dair.

"It's a powerful glamor. Someone has taken a great deal of time to keep this area secret and protected," he whispered, and nerves hummed to life in my chest. This would be where we found Jack, if anywhere. He activated his ear-piece and relayed the intel, but all I heard back was static. Yeah, that wasn't good. Apparently, Jai had been right about the human tech failing at some point.

"How do we get past this, then?" I asked, exploring its solidity with my fingers. I doubted we'd be lucky enough to meet a pair of bumbling guards again. He turned in a full circle and scanned the darkness around us.

"I don't like not knowing what's on the other side. I may have to break the barrier," he said finally. "Once I do, be ready to run, because it'll draw a huge goddamn crowd." I bounced on my toes, my nerves strumming. He still hadn't made any mention of sensing Jack, and I was growing suspicious. This was obviously an Underbelly Circus camp, but it was seeming more and more likely that Jack wasn't there and we were too far into a complicated trap.

For all we knew, there could be an army watching and waiting for us behind this glamor.

"Hello?" A voice called out in the night, from the direction of the still very empty field. I grimaced, really fucking nervous about the idea of this barrier being like a two-way mirror. "I see you in the shadows there, and I can feel your magic. What do you want? I can probably help you."

Dair and I glanced at each other, and I could tell we were both wondering how much of a shit show this would turn out to be.

"If you can't see me, then you need to break the glamor. If you can see me but can't reach me, you need to break the barrier." The voice sounded very young to me. Almost like a child.

I wondered if Killian could see past this glamor. I wished again that I'd had a chance to test a little of

Killian's magic. Even though I knew he wasn't about to touch me, having his skill would have been very useful for tonight's work. Especially since our communication seemed completely dead now.

"Phone?" I whispered to Dair. He slipped his cell from a zippered pocket and scowled, holding it up for me to see. No service. I tried my ear-piece one more time, but there was still nothing. Goddamn it. I didn't like this at all.

"Is that Carlyle, the new girl with the white hair?" The young boy's voice called again. I startled and stumbled into Dair, my eyes growing wide. Adrenaline shot through my veins, and I had to fight to keep myself from bolting. Dair pressed a hand to my shoulder, steadying me.

"My name's Austin. I can hear some of your thoughts, and a few times I've seen you in my dreams. I know that sounds creepy." A boyish giggle followed. "The Ringmaster will be here very soon, so you need to make a decision. If you can't break the glamor or the barrier, then you'll just have to wait for him."

"Austin?" Dair surprised me by calling back to the boy. "Do you know Jack?"

"Of course. He gives me candy, and I give him secrets. Sometimes."

I smiled, feeling less threatened - this kid was funny. I wished I had some candy to give him. "Is Jack here?" I called.

The kid replied, "You shouldn't have come here yet. You're not going to make it this time."

"What?" That sounded bad. Fear sizzled across my shoulders, and I imagined I heard something creaking toward us in the distant darkness of the empty field. Things were out there, and we couldn't even see them.

"You won't make it out of Underbelly alive. None of us will." His voice had dropped to nearly a whisper, but he didn't sound sad, just detached from his fate. This made me desperate to get the kid out of here - he needed some fucking hope in his life besides the promise of death. He needed to play on a playground and eat so much candy he got sick.

"What am I doing - when you see me in your dreams?" I asked, surprising myself with the question.

"Burning," Austin said clearly. "Burning everything down."

Whoa. That was *not* what I'd been suspecting.

"But sometimes my dreams are wrong," he said, the childish warning not enough to buoy my hopes.

"Carlyle?" His voice held dueling notes of fear and rising panic.

"Yes, Austin," I called back. "I'm here."

"I think Jack is going to choose Liberty. Don't let him! He's my friend."

"What is Liberty?" Dair asked, his voice dark and low.

There was no answer for several long seconds, then, "He's here."

The word ended in a strangled noise, and the scrabbling of fingernails against wood. I smacked my fist uselessly into the barrier, knowing Austin was in trouble, but Dair yanked me away, back down into the shadows.

CHAPTER THIRTY-FOUR

CARLYLE

"Hello, Carlyle," a man's voice boomed. I ground my teeth - I hated not being able to see who was seeing me. "Don't you know, poor Jack is on the rack because of you. He jumped his candlestick and got burned, burned, burned."

My heart thudded in my chest. It didn't take a pair of eyes or a rocket scientist to tell me this voice was attached to the Ringmaster, and it didn't take a Jack Nicholson movie to tell me he was a psychopath.

"Well, aren't you going to show yourself and shake my hand? So rude, young people these days. I thought you grew up learning good Southern manners."

I gulped - LuAnn had been very Southern. I realized the Ringmaster had known all along where I'd been. Why hadn't he snatched me years ago? I worked hard to control my heavy breathing as my body fought to flee from this threat. Austin's warning had thrown me into a near panic. I'd escaped Underbelly before, but I might not tonight.

Dair circled my shoulders against his chest. "We can do this, Cariño," he whispered, just as something shimmered across the field, and the glamor lifted.

My stomach bottomed out, and I gasped as I took in the true monstrosity that was Underbelly Circus - a huge gold and green tent loomed in the distance. Smoky torches glowed with fire at the many entrances to the big top and several smaller sideshow tents.

Then my vision tunneled down to the tall man standing before us. He was dressed all in black, with satin stripes up his tuxedo pants and long tails on his coat. The expected top hat and a slim black cane completed the stereotype almost too perfectly. All I could see of his face was a maniacal grin - the hat's brim was too wide and low for anything else.

Dair nudged me, calling my attention beyond the man I'd feared for years, and I realized that between us and the circus tents were rows and rows of cages.

Cages.

Filled with silent, vacant-eyed children and teenagers.

Okay, fuck those people singing sexy kumbaya around the campfire. This place was so going down. I didn't know if it was my special Qilin desire to help, or if it was just the massively fucked-up idea of keeping kids in cages, but I could totally see Austin's dream coming true.

As soon as these kids were free, I would absolutely burn this place to the ground.

"The barrier is still up," Dair whispered, catching my

hand as I moved instinctively toward the cages. I felt the electricity of his magic spark between our fingers, and I wondered how hard it would be to take the Ringmaster down, right fucking now.

"We came for Jack," I announced, since I doubted our plan was any kind of secret.

"Yes, and he came for you. What lovely parallelism. But what goes up must come down. Jack jumped for you, but you haven't flown for me. Do you have your wings yet, pretty Qilin?" He repeated the last two words over and over, muttering like someone would to a pet bird.

"Hey, cuckoo for cocoa puffs!" I yelled, interrupting the weirdo and hoping my voice stayed steady. "Where's Jack?" I lifted a fist and felt in front of me until I found the barrier again, then I smacked it a few times. Which did nothing, of course, except sting my hand a little. I felt Dair hovering just behind me, and I sensed his soft, exploratory magic.

The Ringmaster grinned and leaned against the back of the nearest cage, which probably held an unconscious or dead kid named Austin. God, I hated feeling so helpless.

The odd creaking noise from before was growing louder, and I pressed into the barrier, struggling to see through the darkness between the cages. The bright fires beyond made it that much harder, but suddenly I focused on a large, wooden wheel rolling toward us. There was something tied to it. No... *someone.*

"Dair?" I muttered, canting my head. He squinted, but we both realized at the same second exactly what we were seeing. My heart flared with rage and sorrow, and I prayed we weren't too fucking late. Dair roared and shot a bolt of pure white magic into the barrier. I copied his words and added what I could, hoping to fissure this invisible dome so we could rescue their poor, bloodied teammate.

The Ringmaster only cackled in glee as the barrier held, and he beckoned to the figure pushing the wheel. "Closer, my beauty! Faster, for Jack has missed his friends so!"

Jack was lashed to the giant wheel, arms and legs spread-eagled against a gaudy, sequined star. All around him, sunk deep in the wood, were dozens of throwing knives. He was dressed in only a pair of ripped, blood-stained jeans, and his flesh was ragged, covered in still-oozing knife slashes and sooty, burned patches. As the wheel moved, it also rotated, turning his limp body around and around in a sickening, dizzy circle.

Dair grunted and pushed even more power into the barrier, but I could tell he was losing the edge of his strength. Mine didn't seem to be helping at all, so I backed off. I didn't know anything about this psychopath's powers, and I needed to reserve what I could. So did Dair, I realized, and I tugged at his arm.

"Get a grip," I whispered to the mage, my voice furious. "Jack?" I yelled to the unmoving form strung on the wheel. He had to be alive, dammit. I may have cursed him and hated him after he'd tricked and trapped me, but that was before I realized how much he'd been trapped. Now, I thought of him as one of the team - *my* team.

We weren't going anywhere without him.

"Jack!" I screamed as Dair continued to pummel the barrier. The Ringmaster just watched us and twirled his goddamn stick and giggled like a psychopath.

Jack's eyelids flickered, but never fully opened, and my throat closed up as I scanned the bruises and gashes that covered every inch of his skin. A single knife was embedded to the hilt in his abdomen.

He would survive, though - he had to. He'd jumped off a bridge and lived, for fuck's sake.

The wheel finally came to a rest, and a small figure stepped from behind it, dressed all in black and sequins, like some sort of macabre assistant. The upper half of her face was covered by an eyeless mask, and her mouth was gagged and bound with a blood-soaked rag. I thought I caught the glimpse of a shiny fang poking over the edge of the cloth, but just then, Dair made a horrible, strangled noise and fell to his knees, his power fizzling away to nothing.

Crying out, he slumped against the barrier as though it were a glass wall, holding him forever apart from the gory scene on the other side.

I knelt next to him, all too fucking aware of the cackling Ringmaster as he watched us like we were putting on a stage show for him. Goddamn, I hated that man. "Dair?"

"Kana," he moaned.

The masked girl jerked her head toward his voice, startling me. She took a single step before crumpling to her knees, screaming past her bloody gag as her palms pressed against her temples.

"Stop!" I shouted, not even understanding what was happening.

"Behave, Kana," the Ringmaster warned, and the girl's screaming lessened, then stopped, as she sobbed quietly on the grass before the wheel. Jack's eyes had finally opened in the commotion, and I saw fear and panic dawn on his face as he saw Dair and me.

"No," he mouthed, twisting pointlessly against his

bindings. A few more of his wounds opened, and I jerked to my feet, holding up a hand.

"Wait, Jack," I called, pressing against the barrier. I needed a second to think - to figure out what the hell was happening. Dair was clawing at the ground as though he now meant to dig beneath the barrier, and the girl had quieted and curled into herself even more. She was sucking at the bloody rag so hard I could hear it, and my stomach churned.

Dair knew her, but who was she?

I saw the glint of fang again. I gasped as she twisted away from me, and I saw her long, ebony hair bound into a thick braid.

"Jai?" I whispered, and she jerked as though someone had kicked her. She had to be a vampire like Jai - and her small size and black hair meant she might even be related to him.

The Ringmaster shouted with glee. "Ha! You solved a riddle! What a good little beastie you are." He clapped his hands, and the invisible magic holding me back vanished. I tumbled to the ground, several feet closer to the Ringmaster's polished black boots.

I swiveled back to reach for Dair, but the barrier snapped in place behind me.

Ah, fuck. Now I was trapped inside. I reached for a knife to cut the psycho open, only to find all my weapons and tech had somehow been chafed away and left on the other side of the barrier. Double fuck.

"Go find the others," I roared to Dair, my voice carrying more force than any goddamn Alpha's ever could. I wasn't about to let him lose another brother over me.

Dair's eyes widened, and he blinked at me twice, then obediently popped out of existence.

CHAPTER THIRTY-FIVE

CARLYLE

"How fun," the Ringmaster murmured, grinning at the three of us in turn - the dark-haired girl who looked way too much like Jai to be a fucking coincidence, and Jack, who was probably dying an agonizing and, frankly, embarrassing death.

Yeah, I was done.

Drawing myself up, I shoved all I had against the man's face - all of Dair's magic and Sol's strength in one giant bitch-slap.

He stumbled backward into a cage, his face whipping so far back I was hopeful I'd snapped his neck.

I rushed at Jack, clambering up the edges of the wheel and shaking his shoulders. He was slipping in and out of consciousness. I used the embedded knives like climbing handles, and when one came free in my hands, I turned and hurled it at the Ringmaster, who was rubbing at his cheek with wide, wondrous eyes.

He ducked, of course.

"Carlyle," Jack whispered, and I whipped my gaze back to him. Our faces were so close I could kiss him right now, and suddenly that's exactly what I wanted to do, more than anything. I had a tiny sizzle of magic left - maybe I could channel it into him. "You came... I wanted it. But... shouldn't have."

His eyes started to slide closed again, and I pressed my lips to his. I was desperate to shove any shreds of magic or energy straight into him. His eyes struggled open again, and one side of his lips hooked up.

"So fucking strong," he mumbled, the words slurred.

I grabbed his cheeks, trying to keep him looking at me. "Listen to me, Jack. Your brothers are here. They're coming for you."

"Brothers?" he mumbled, as though the word were foreign. My stomach flipped - had he gone so rogue he didn't even remember his team?

Hooking one arm around his shoulder for balance, I started yanking at the ropes lashing his arms to the wheel.

"I told you she was special, didn't I," the Ringmaster's great, booming voice rang out behind me. I grunted, snapping one rope, only to have it weave itself back together. Rage filled my vision - stupid fucking magic. I didn't know a spell for that, and I probably didn't have enough power to do one, anyway. I grabbed a knife and began sawing at the rope again.

"Carlyle, go. Get out of here," Jack whispered into my

hair, sounding frantic. "Don't let him win."

The Ringmaster's heavy hand had already circled the back of my neck, and I froze. He hauled me off Jack way too easily, sending me sprawling down onto the grass. The knife bounced away into the thick grass.

"Your brothers are so weak still. So useless to me," the man said, a sneer twisting his lips. He waved a dismissive hand, and I scrambled around to see Dair, Sol, and Killian at the outside edge of the barrier, each of their hands locked to their skulls as pain contorted their faces. The masked girl had resumed her similar position, moaning and grinding her teeth.

"Stop! What are you doing to them?" I yelled, darting to my feet and flying at the Ringmaster with my fists ready. He dodged my blows without even working for it, and I cursed myself for being too weak, too inexperienced.

"I'm reminding these boys who's still in charge," he hissed, grabbing a handful of my braid and turning my back to his front. Pain seared through my scalp. "They might be in line to rule Haret, but here on Earth, my power trumps everything!"

I balked at his claim that my guys were rulers, but that was so not the point right now. He was slowly crumpling each of them into an unrecognizable mush of man. I had to do something, but I had no weapons. No magic.

This was the same position Sol had been training me in, but his grip on my hair was too tight. My feet were skidding too much in the dusty grass for me to get a good stance to kick backward.

"If you're so powerful, how come none of that magic is affecting me?" I taunted to distract him, hoping he wouldn't call my bluff. I really didn't want to experience whatever skull-shattering trick he was doing with the guys. Gritting my teeth against his hair-pulling - honestly, it felt so much better when Dair did it - I let myself grow still so he'd think I was done fighting.

"You're a cipher, pretty little Qilin," he cooed in my ear. "A beautiful, delicate, empty vessel just waiting to be *filled.*"

I almost threw up in my mouth, hoping he was way too old to think about filling any part of me. Who was I kidding? Earth was full of skeevy perverts, so probably Haret was too.

"So your mind magic doesn't work on me?" I asked, cutting to what I hoped was the kernel of truth.

"No, it doesn't," he ground out, his fingers twisting even tighter in my hair and making me grit out a tiny scream. "Which is why I'm so thankful you brought friends for me to play with."

Beyond the barrier, my three guys slumped completely over, their bodies going motionless in the dark grass.

Just then, my heel finally caught in a clump of grass, giving me the leverage I needed. I screamed in rage, shoving my other boot straight back into his groin, the way Sol had taught me. The Ringmaster's fingers loosened just enough. I ducked to yank my braid free, throwing a wild sideways punch into his gut. He lurched back, thrown off balance.

I darted toward Jack again. I didn't even bother with the ropes, instead tugging another knife free and hurling it at the Ringmaster.

It clipped his stupid top hat right off his fucking head, and I smirked, already going for another.

Jack gurgled then, and I knew I was almost out of time.

He was going to die. Even though I knew he'd come back to life somehow before, I had no idea if he could do it again or what it would cost him.

"Kana," he rasped, and the girl on the ground trembled. "My scale. Please," he begged. I snapped another knife back at the Ringmaster, who caught it between his fingers, flipping it around in his hand. Ah, shit.

I wasn't as good at dodging as I was at throwing. I grabbed two more knives.

"What do you want from us?" I called to the Ringmaster, hoping to get him talking again and stall for whatever Jack wanted from Kana. I slid off the wheel and stepped toward the Ringmaster again. I held my knives at the ready, keeping myself between him and Jack. I didn't think he wanted me dead, so maybe I could be their shield.

Kana crawled on the grass behind me, and I hoped she knew what she was doing. I dodged and ducked, keeping the Ringmaster's beady eyes on me instead of them.

"I want what I've always wanted," the Ringmaster said, flipping the knife through his fingers like a card trick now. His voice was terrifyingly calm. "Now, I have those three, and the other one sneaking around near my tents, trying to find what I've hidden. This one," he nodded at Jack, "and that just leaves the mer-king. Lions and fairies and mermaids, oh my!" he cackled. "I'll take a piece of each - why choose when you can have them all, right Qilin?"

"Fuck off," I answered eloquently. Behind me, Jack cried out, and I risked a glance back to see what the hell Kana was up to. Maybe she'd gone rogue, too.

"Oh, no you don't," the Ringmaster cried, sounding worried for the first time. Kana lunged at me, shoving something deep in my pocket as we went down on the grass, rolling until I was on top of her. In the scuffle, I lost one of my knives.

"What did you do?" I yelled at her, pushing my remaining blade to her throat. I wanted to tear the mask off her face and look straight into her eyes, but its strings were woven tightly into her hair.

Jack was bleeding even worse now - had she cut him open?

She struggled beneath me, shoving me away with surprising strength. As I pushed up, she stumbled into a weak, blind run, getting maybe a dozen shaky steps before her body was flung sideways. She smacked into the invisible barrier with a crack of bones and a sickening squish of organs.

I swiveled back to the Ringmaster, my eyes wide and flicking between his crazed grin and Jack's slumped head. Surely Kana was dead. Jack was only seconds behind - I could feel it, somehow.

I glanced back to my guys. None of them were moving either, and blood was trickling out of their noses.

Everyone was dying, and I had no idea how to save them.

The Ringmaster surged forward, smacking my last weapon out of my hand. He snatched my arm and dragged me closer to the wheel. He caught my other hand and twisted both arms behind my back and up, yanking until my muscles screamed. If only I'd had more of Sol's strength, or more of Dair's magic.

I had nothing - no power left. I promised myself if I got out of here, I would train every motherfucking day.

I would ruin this man.

"Well, Jack," he said, chuckling, "I should ask you if you want Life or Liberty now, shouldn't I? Before you burn out again? For everything, burn, burn, burn. There is a season, burn, burn, burn," he sang, butchering the words to a really nice song.

I recognized the word Liberty from Austin's rambling. "Jack, choose Life! Jack!"

His head lolled to the side, his eyes fluttering open.

The Ringmaster cackled. "It's not much of a choice for an immortal dragon! Of course, you'll choose Life. Life chooses you!"

"Liberty," Jack rasped, trying to rouse. "I choose Liberty!" he yelled, the force of the words pushing more blood out of his many wounds.

"Goddamn it! He wants Life," I yelled, interrupting him and struggling harder against the iron grip on my arms.

The Ringmaster sighed as though all of this were just too much fucking work. "Oh, Jack. This form isn't quite so nimble or quick. If you wanted to break your contract, you should have listened to the girl and chosen better."

A scream ripped from my throat as the Ringmaster stopped flipping the knife and threw it effortlessly, straight into Jack's heart. The point thudded all the way through his flesh and into the wood behind him. Blood began to pour from his mouth as he choked on the thick red liquid.

I fought as hard as I could against the Ringmaster, but he held me with inhuman strength and a flare of magic, tunneling a hand into my braid again and forcing me to watch as Jack bled out in seconds.

"No," I wailed, cringing as my scalp burned and my shoulder joints ached. I tried to throw my head back to break his nose, but it only thudded onto his chest - I was too short. I flailed and kicked a leg back, but he sidestepped. I bucked against his hold, pain be damned.

"Burn, burn, burn," the Ringmaster began to sing again, his voice childlike as he kept my body locked against his. "Jack be nimble, Jack be quick. Jack fell down and broke his crown. Oh, look, Jack is dead!"

As the words soaked into my brain, Jack's body erupted into flames, disintegrating in moments and taking the wooden wheel with it, until all that was left before me was a pile of ash drifting on the summer night's breeze.

CHAPTER THIRTY-SIX

CARLYLE

"I hope he chooses a better name next time," the Ringmaster said, his voice light as he tried to pull me away from the smoking pile that used to be Jack.

I dug my heels into the grass. He'd have to pull every fucking strand of hair from my head.

Thank God that didn't happen, though. We both twisted around as a groan sounded behind us. Sol was up and rubbing at his temples, and Killian crawled behind the shield of his stronger friend. The Ringmaster must have dropped his control over them while he dealt with Jack.

The moon rolled behind a cloud. I couldn't see Dair very well, but when the barrier began to ripple and creak like a house in a windstorm, I grinned. I sensed the magic pouring from Killian, joining Dair's and strengthening it.

They were going to break the barrier down. My guys weren't dead or beaten - not at all.

The barrier flickered with brief light, and a wave undulated across its surface like a sea monster rising on a still lake. It burst, lightning flaring across the sky and the air popping so loudly around us that I went deaf for several seconds. Blinking away the bright spots in my vision, I saw their mouths open and yelling, and I felt the impact of someone smashing into me, but I couldn't hear a damn thing.

The Ringmaster's hold on my hair and arms was broken, and someone scooped me up and sped me away so fast everything was a blur.

Then the air popped around me, and I rolled to my side, vomiting onto a cold tile floor.

Two more pops sounded, and Killian was there. Pop, pop, then Sol. Then Jai and Dair.

Never Jack.

We'd failed - so epically I could barely believe it. Jack was dead, and the Ringmaster knew how weak we were.

The room tilted around me as I tried to stand, and I felt Sol's warm skin as he pulled me close. "Shortcake," he murmured against my hair, his arms tight around my waist. My brain spun, and the only coherent thought I managed was that I hoped he didn't kiss me, because I tasted like puke.

"Jack," I croaked, and someone handed me a glass of water. I blinked down at it - I wanted fucking Jack, not a goddamn glass of water.

"Get it together, kid." Killian's harsh voice cut through

my haze. I swiveled my head until I located him, glaring at me. I imagined flipping him off, but I was just too tired to bother.

Sol maneuvered me to a chair at the dining table, and I focused with difficulty on the body before me.

Oh yeah, there was a body on the table.

Jai was bent over the girl, his entire body coiled like a cobra. I stretched my fingers to his, careful not to startle him, and as soon as our skin touched, my nose was flooded with grave-mud sorrow and the heady, steam and crackle of barn-burning rage.

Sol covered my fingers, pressing them down on Jai's. Killian joined us at Jai's other side, and Dair reached up wearily from the chair he was slumped in. All of us laid hands on our leader as he mourned the young woman on the table where we'd so recently gathered as a team. As a family.

"Forgive me, Kana," he whispered, his voice so broken I nearly lost my mind. Fucking hell, this family shit was brutal.

I'd never gotten close enough to anyone before to feel this way about them, but goddamn if my heart wasn't breaking along with my guys'.

I don't know if it was minutes or hours later, but we all slumped into the chairs around the table, Kana's body still before us like we were at some sort of twisted visitation service. I kept sneaking glances at Dair - he'd sort of passed out, and his skin was much too pale.

None of the others seemed worried about him, though, so I tried to focus on what was left.

"What happened to Jack?" I finally asked, breaking the heavy silence. I knew all my guys were beating themselves up for a failed mission, but I had to know.

"He'll be born again. The same as always," Killian muttered, scrubbing at his face with both hands. "Not Kana."

Jai's fingers stroked along Kana's pale, limp hand. Someone had removed her mask, though her eyes were closed. Now that I could see her face, there was no mistaking the resemblance between her and Jai.

In a flat voice, he explained, "The magic in Jack's dragon scales allows him to regenerate each time his human form fails."

"Too bad you didn't fuck him, too," Killian growled, jumping up from the table and slamming out the back door to the deck. I heard a roar of anger, but all I could do was stare in shock. The fuck was his problem?

Dair groaned awake and scrubbed his hands over his face.

Sol leaned close. "I'm sorry, Carlyle. He feels guilty - we all do. But he shouldn't take it out on you. None of us even knew Kana was on Earth."

I nodded, but something was squirming in my brain, trying to unearth itself from the dirt of exhaustion and failure. "I could have taken Jack's power?"

"Yes," Jai agreed, a sad smile crossing his lips for just a second. "You could channel Jack's power just as you can Sol's, or any of ours. He is lost to us now, until his soul reforms his body. It is too late."

I shook away the confusion of whatever that meant - I wasn't done. That thing in my brain was still squirming, and I grabbed its tail to haul the idea into the light. Standing, I shoved my hand in my pants pocket, finding the tiny, sharp thing Kana had shoved there just before she was killed.

I drew it out and stared at it resting in the palm of my hand. It was a scale, smooth and glistening and perfect. A magical fucking dragon regeneration scale, if I was understanding all of this correctly.

"Holy fuck, Cariño," Dair slurred, ending on a slightly hysterical laugh as he leaned over to see what I held. Sol joined him, and I flinched as Jai snatched the scale from my hand so fast I barely saw him move. He leaped like a cat right onto the table and tore open Kana's black shirt, revealing massive bruising and several lumps around her ribs that really shouldn't be there.

Sol handed Jai a knife, and I cried out as Jai sliced Kana's chest wide open, digging his fingers deep into her flesh. I stumbled away from the table, horrified and slightly sick. I mean, I trusted them, but what the hell were they even doing?

Jai's fingers slid out of her chest cavity, smeared to the wrist with blood and fisted around something I had to force myself to look at.

Dair breathed a curse as Jai set the bloody object on the table and inserted the scale into it.

I crept forward a tiny bit. It was... a box? Why did this chick have a box in her chest?

These Haretians so owed me an explanation.

Jai pushed the box carefully back into her chest, and within seconds, her skin began to knit itself together again. I gasped as the lumps smoothed themselves out and the bruising faded. Her chest began to rise and fall with breath, and she moaned, her eyelids fluttering.

Jai bent his forehead to hers, gathering her shoulders tight to him and breathing her name over and over.

I felt tears prick behind my eyes. She was alive.

Jack had known what the Ringmaster would do - what he was capable of doing. He'd asked Kana to get a scale just for this very reason. My own chest heaved as I fell a little in love with the odd dragon shifter from the bridge.

He was crazy, yeah, but anyone who could think about a thing like that while in that much pain? He could have my heart, wherever he was.

I felt Sol slide his arms around me and pull me close for a hug. "You saved the day, shortcake," he whispered, his voice thick as he nuzzled my hair.

"Who is she?" I asked, just to be sure.

"Jai's sister," Sol said. Dair flicked his eyes to us, overhearing the words. His gaze flew to the back door, and he bellowed Killian's name.

"And Killian's fiancée," Sol finished as the door slammed again and Killian burst into the room, his eyes wild as he fixed an unbelieving stare on Kana. Her eyes fluttered, and she coughed weakly. Jai wiped away a bit of blood from her lips, then Killian was on the table too, burying his face in her neck, his shoulders shaking as he gathered her close. Jai's arms circled both of them, pressing their trio together.

I took a step back into Sol, feeling like I'd been slapped.

Fiancée? Well, at least that explained the kid comments. Suddenly feeling like I was intruding, I hurried from the kitchen and pounded up the stairs to my room.

CHAPTER THIRTY-SEVEN

CARLYLE

I locked my door and slid down its slick surface, my head in my hands.

It shouldn't bother me that Killian had a fiancée. I didn't need all the fucking men to myself. I was being goddamn ridiculous even feeling slighted by this new development.

A girl had just been brought back to life with a dragon scale, for fuck's sake.

As I lashed myself over and over in my mind, trying to exorcise the demon that still insisted Killian should be mine, I heard a scuffle and scrape at the window.

Wait. The window? I was on the second floor. My heart started to pound.

Rising, I pressed myself into the wall and slid closer, keeping just out of sight of whatever was out there. With my luck, the Ringmaster or one of his flying monkeys had followed us home. I didn't hear any of the guys outside my room - they were probably all still having a great fucking family reunion downstairs. The scratching at the window intensified, and the pane began to rattle like a storm was brewing.

I saw a flash of garnet, though, and my heart jumped as I hurried closer, my nose honing in on the smell of smoke and fire.

"Jack?" I pressed my face to the windowpane. A huge shape hovered beyond, enormous wings stretched across the night sky. The moon was brighter here than at the circus, and as the creature banked, I saw its deep red hue clearly in the silvery light.

I fumbled with the window lock and shoved it open, leaning out into the night air. "Jack?" I repeated, feeling a little foolish.

I mean, hopefully there weren't too many other red freaking dragons out there.

The beast turned its wide snout to me, its tongue lolling out the side in what looked like a goofy sort of dog grin. I shrieked as it snorted and crowded into the open window, but then its bulk began to deflate and shrink like a popped balloon, until my room was filled not with a dragon, but with a grinning man.

He fixed his gaze on me, his bright, ice-blue eyes flashing behind thick, dark lashes. God, I'd forgotten how beautiful he was.

I hesitated, suddenly shy. "How are you here?" I managed. And *why*, I wanted to ask. I mean, talk about the most confusing man ever.

His smile faded a bit. "I'm so sorry, Carlyle. About everything. I meant what I said on the bridge that night. Life and death really are the same to me. My body can die, but my dragon soul always builds it back again. I can build any body I want, but I made this one again so I wouldn't scare you."

"This is a nice one," I said, then slapped my fingers over my mouth. So inappropriate, when he was trying to be all sensitive and shit.

His grin grew into a hungry sort of smirk, and he took a step forward, then another, crowding me against the bed when I didn't push him away. "I asked you not to let me down," he whispered. I could feel the flare of his body heat without even touching him. "And you didn't. You were fucking brilliant back there." He leaned in, his breath flaming across my neck.

All I wanted was to give in and let him kiss away the whole awful fucking night, but I had one more question. "What's Liberty?"

His eyes shuttered, and he drew back. Ah, dammit. I bit at my lips too late - always ruining the mood.

"He always asks them to pick Life or Liberty. When they pick Life, he gets their magic."

"And they stay alive?"

Jack glared. "If you can call it that. But I knew I'd be alive either way. Now I'm free." His smile returned, but something about it was forced. I thought of all those cages. All those kids. I thought I knew why his eyes were so haunted.

"We'll get them all out," I said on impulse, and the blue of his eyes turned almost black as his eyes dilated.

"You," he breathed, a growl beginning low in his belly. He surged against me, his mouth hot and harsh and fucking amazing against mine. Coming up for air, he said, "You're so strong, and I fucking love it." He sucked a tender spot behind my ear, and my legs grew weak. I buckled onto the bed, and Jack pushed his way between my knees, capturing my face between his palms.

He nuzzled against me, pressing me onto my back while he hovered above me. His stubble scratched against my cleavage as he kissed his way up and down my neck. I moaned as his hips ground down into mine, his cock hard between us. Ah, shit, I wanted to be naked with this man.

I stretched my neck up and met his lips, nipping at him with my teeth. He chuckled and traced my lips with his tongue, tasting me and humming in satisfaction. I parted my lips, inviting him in, and he continued to explore and tease. His hands slipped down my sides, scratching at the slick tactical fabric.

Ugh. It would take hours to get all these clothes off.

I sucked in a gasp as he held a single finger up before me and shifted it into a wicked scythe of a claw, nearly the length of my forearm. The tight fabric of my shirt parted like butter beneath that claw, and I held my breath, afraid to get skewered.

Pulling his dragon back in, he spread his fingers across my chest, slipping them just beneath the black lace of my bra as he kissed closer and closer.

I reached up and tangled my fingers in his scruffy brown hair, hoping to tug him right down to my aching nipples. Clutching at him, I felt my pleasure build, hovering just at the edge between sweet and sexy.

Damn, I wanted a piece of this dragon.

Something crept in behind that thought, though - something important the Ringmaster had said. As much as I really didn't want to kill the mood again, I needed to know one more thing.

"Jack?" I whispered, and he inched his mouth up to meet mine.

"Mmm?" His lips kissed lightly along my jaw.

"What contract did you have with the Ringmaster? What did he take from you?"

The kisses stopped, and Jack's face rose above me, his eyes wary. "What?"

I could tell he'd heard me just fine. "He said he wanted a piece of you - of each of you. What did he take?"

Jack muttered under his breath, rolling onto his back beside me. His hands scrubbed his face, shoving back into his hair and making it stand up all wild and sexy. I propped myself up and stared down at him, my heart pounding as I waited.

His eyes were full of fear, and when I tugged his hand out of his hair, he was shaking with it. He stank of it - dank cages and moldy bread and the sort of stench that comes from not bathing for days on end.

"Jack," I whispered, my chest tight with fear.

"He couldn't have," he said, his words ending on a moan. He fixed his gaze on me, and I trembled at the raw terror there. Panicked and wishing I'd never said anything, I clung to him and sank my mouth onto his, kissing him like I was running out of time instead of just beginning it. He answered me with the same sort of kiss - an end-of-the-line kiss.

A goodbye kiss.

Then his screams filled the room, his body bending

double over me as he gripped his temples in both hands. Trapped beneath his chest, I had access to all his skin - all his turmoil and fear.

It was a million times worse than what I'd felt on the bridge.

"Jack," I yelled, trying to shove between him and himself, but he was lost to the pain inside his head. His body began to flicker and lose shape and substance right before me, as though he were being sucked away into the air. Was he shifting? Siphoning? Did he even have that power?

"Carlyle," he gritted out, suddenly twisting and pinning me beneath him on the bed. His kiss was an act of desperation - a push through unimaginable pain. Still, it was more passionate - more real - than anything I'd ever felt.

My soul seemed to beat its way out of my chest and fuse with his in that moment, and power surged through my veins. I felt like I could live forever.

"Don't let me down," he panted, thrusting the power against me and through me and into me.

I took it all in, like I'd been doing all my life with human emotions. I took his power and his magic and his desire, and I channeled it.

And I *kept* it.

I was a motherfucking vessel, and I was being filled with something precious. I would keep it safe, and when the time came, I would give it back to him with a goddamn vengeance.

"I'm yours whenever you need me," I said, pressing my mouth against the base of his neck. "And you're *mine*," I finished fiercely, even as his body flickered once more and vanished from the room with a hollow pop.

For what seemed like forever, I waited, not moving. Surely the others had heard the screams and would come running. I stayed on my back on the bed, staring up at the plain white ceiling in a daze.

My body had gone from singing with power to little better than numb. My mind was no longer racing but had settled into a steady loop.

Jack was gone again, but he wasn't - because I had my piece of dragon, and we were stronger for it. We would get him back, and soon.

I'd discovered something about myself and about Qilin tonight. Qilin weren't magical taxi cabs, and we weren't party busses, either. We were keepers of the Path, and every path is made of smaller pieces.

I had one piece inside me now, and I had a pretty good idea how to get the others.

I also knew the Ringmaster would stop at nothing to steal everything - why he wanted the Path all to himself was a mystery, but I didn't care. I'd do whatever it took to stop him.

Forcing myself to my feet, I peeled off the ruined black shirt and shimmied out of my pants, replacing both with the soft knit leggings and cream sweater Dair had given me. Staring at myself in the mirror, I realized I looked different.

It wasn't like in cheesy movies where gaining magic makes you more beautiful. There was something truly other-worldly about me now. Something Haretian.

Something *Qilin*.

Turning my face from side to side in the mirror and examining my neck, I peered closer, gaping when I discovered a distinct, visible shimmer to my skin. When the light hit me in just the right way, that shimmer gathered into something more solid.

Scales.

I laughed out loud as I realized what I was looking at - my skin shone and undulated with patches of overlapping garnet scales. They slipped in and out of existence, but they were there, they were badass, and they were fucking gorgeous.

I pivoted on my heel and bounded down the stairs, my stomach churning at the idea of telling the guys everything that had just happened.

CHAPTER THIRTY-EIGHT

CARLYLE

When I skidded to a stop in the living room doorway and took in the scene, though, I felt instantly like an intruder again.

Kana was on the couch, sandwiched between Jai and Killian. Now that she wasn't all dead, I could see exactly how amazingly beautiful she was, with huge midnight eyes and perfect skin. Dair was sprawled in the chair I usually took, and Sol had stretched flat on the floor.

My guys were gathered around her like metal to a magnet.

"Ah," I started, and everyone turned to look at me. The guys just stared, and for the life of me, I couldn't read a single one of them. I took a step backward.

Kana shot off the couch, startling a cry from my lips. She was before me in an instant, stunning me stupid. I blinked at her.

"Thank you," she said, her voice soft but forceful. It reminded me a lot of Jai's. My hands grew cold, and I looked down, realizing she had my fingers grasped in hers.

"Ah, no problem," I managed. "Are you okay?"

She grinned, letting a flash of fang show. "I'm fucking great."

I choked out a surprised laugh, though I still didn't have any idea what to think of her being here. I'd just been figuring out my place in the group, and now I had to worry about another girl in the mix. I tried to tamp down the jealousy, but I was losing big time.

"No, seriously. Thank you," Kana repeated, squeezing my hand again. "I just knew I was going to die in that hellhole. The Ringmaster had me drugged, constantly." She shuddered. "It was on that rag - my fangs can't help but suck on the blood like a reflex. The drug kept my muscles from moving at normal speed, and it gave me hallucinations. I didn't trust my own senses. When Jack showed up, I didn't even believe it was him."

"Did he recruit you?" I asked, wondering how far back his job went.

"No," she bit out. "We need to go back for him, though." She turned and glared at Jai, and I sensed this was an argument they'd already begun.

"It's too dangerous right now," Jai said wearily. "We don't even know if Jack has regenerated yet."

"Ah, he has," I said, twisting my fingers away from hers. I felt heat settle in my cheeks as five pairs of eyes fixed on me. No, six pairs.

"Holy shit," Sol said, rising fluidly to his feet and approaching me slowly. He stretched out a hand, keeping eye contact like he was afraid I was a rabid dog or something. "Look," he whispered, feathering a finger across my exposed shoulder. The others crowded around me until I was in a circle of sexy men.

Ah, and Killian's fiancée. Right.

"Explain," Dair ordered, his eyes blazing with curiosity as his fingers slipped over my scale-spotted skin.

I related the previous half hour or so as coherently as I could, which was damn difficult, as I barely understood what had happened.

"So I'm pretty sure he's back at the circus, but I have the magic the Ringmaster wanted," I finished.

"You figured it out with raw instinct," Jai said, his voice quiet with awe.

Kana giggled. "I never thought Jack would be the first one mated."

My head snapped toward her, and I heard one of the guys curse. "Mated?" I repeated, my eyes narrowing as my brain kicked on. So that's what stealing a piece of Jack meant. Ah, fuck.

"Oh, hell to the fucking no. You guys didn't tell her?" Kana's voice was getting a little screechy, and before I knew it, she'd wrapped her arm around me and hauled me outside onto the deck. She slammed the door shut so hard the windows rattled, and the look she sent back at the guys warned them not to move a muscle.

"What did I do?" I asked her. "Mate with Jack?"

"Afraid so. I mean, it's not bad. Jack's awesome when he's not being an asshole because of the Ringmaster. But you should not have been going into that blind." Her voice pulsed with anger.

"They told me I should figure out my Qilin nature, ah, naturally. Like they didn't want to tell me Qilin craved sweets and sex. They wanted me to figure it out."

Kana snorted. "Every girl craves sweets and sex. Fucking morons," she raged.

I laughed, and it felt good. The stress of the night had taken a huge toll, and as much as we'd won with Kana, we'd also lost way too much. I was worn down, like when I'd taken in too many depressing emotions on a festival work night. I needed the physical relief of laughter.

Orgasm wouldn't hurt either, especially after that hot makeout session with Jack.

"Ah, what do I do now? About Jack?" I asked, trying to focus.

She shrugged. "I can't tell you that. I do know the others will be lining up, though. Now that you've committed to one, you're in trouble, girl."

"Have you and Killian mated?" I was such a glutton for punishment.

Kana leveled her black eyes at me and arched an eyebrow. "Are you fucking kidding me?"

My mouth popped open and closed like a fish, and her face pinched together. "Ah... "

"Killian!" She roared his name, startling several sleeping birds from the woods beyond the deck. The redhead opened the door a few seconds later and sauntered over to us, leaning his back against the railing. He crossed his arms over his chest, the action pushing out his considerable muscles.

"Yes, love?"

"Tell this girl the goddamn truth," Kana demanded.

His eyes hardened, his cheeks flushing red. "Which one, love?"

I narrowed my eyes at the tone he'd turned on her, but she only huffed.

"She asked if we're mated, you dick-for-brains."

Killian simmered, and for a moment, I thought he was going to refuse her whatever she was asking. Her eyes were locked on his in an unrelenting demand, and he finally shrugged.

"No, we are na mated."

"Because…" she prompted.

"Because Kana is racist," he finished, flashing her a sneer.

"Oh, for fuck's sake." She threw her hands up in the air and turned back to me. "What he's trying to say is our mating was arranged - and neither of us wants any part in it."

"Why?" I had to ask. This was turning into the kind of show I wanted popcorn for, though a tiny part of me was doing a victory dance that Killian wasn't spoken for, after all.

"For starters, I don't like redheads." Kana stalked toward Killian, menace on her face. He squared his shoulders as if preparing to fight her off. I pushed off the railing, ready to help or get out of the way, as needed. Then she grinned viciously. "And for finishers, I don't like cocky fae or fae cock."

"That's likely because you've never had fae cock," Killian jeered, but he was grinning, too.

"Oh, I've had it," she taunted. She glanced at me and winked. "And it's nothing compared to what vampire cock can do." She wiggled her little finger mockingly at him. He growled, and she stepped right up to his chest, barely reaching his shoulders. They scuffled lightly, ending with her clinging to his back, her fangs in a precarious position on his jugular.

"I give up, me," he said, laughter spilling into the night.

"Asshole," she said, grinning as she hopped down and shoved her shoulder into his. "Kills and I have been friends longer than you've been alive, Qilin. But rest easy knowing we'll never be lovers."

I shrugged as though it didn't matter, but as I turned away, I caught the edge of Killian's glare, and my stomach flipped. I wasn't sure how much longer I could lie to myself.

The door opened behind us, and the others filed out, their faces much too grim for the mood on the deck.

"What is it?" I asked.

Jai took a deep breath. "If Jack's been here, we have to leave. He'll have been followed."

"New safe house?" I said, my heart sinking.

"New safe house," Dair affirmed, holding out his hand. He already had a leather satchel over his shoulder. "Come here, Cariño. I want you to see it first."

I groaned, holding my belly. Not more siphoning. He gathered me into his arms gently, bending to kiss the top of my head before the familiar spinning sensation began.

My feet landed easily, though, and I glanced up at him in surprise.

"That was better!"

"Jack's magic steadied you," he murmured, turning me in his arms so my back was pressed against his chest. I gasped at the view spread before me - miles and miles of crystal blue ocean, and the most beautiful fucking sunrise a girl could ask for, spilling orange and hot pink and shades of purple all down the rippling water.

"Thank you," I whispered, turning my face up to look at Dair.

He smiled and pressed a gentle kiss to my forehead. "You deserve a nice beach vacation. Besides, I hear there's a magnificent four-poster bed inside that house, just waiting for a good girl to claim it."

A thrill shot straight through me as he trailed his lips down the bridge of my nose, pecking at my lips like the freaking tease he was.

"Now, can you be persuaded to wait just a bit?" He dropped the satchel at my feet.

"Will it be worth it?" I teased back.

His eyes flared, and he brushed his lips against mine so lightly I could barely feel it. "It's always worth it, Cariño." His arms slipped from mine, and he popped out of the air, leaving me alone on the white sand.

I breathed in deeply of the salt and sea, grinning into the rising sun. I'd waited my whole life for a family like this.

A few more minutes wouldn't hurt.

WANT MORE?

Find Laurel and the Piece of Dragon fans in the Facebook
reader group LOVERS OF HARET.
https://www.facebook.com/groups/676410892715276/

Join Laurel's newsletter for new release information, sales,
and special, sexy bonus content.
https://mailchi.mp/b5909ca75df1/piece-of-dragon

REVIEWS

Please consider leaving an honest review on your favorite
reading and retail sites.
Lots of readers depend on reviews and recommendations
to find their next read.

Love, Laurel

LaurelChaseAuthor.com

PIECE OF DRAGON

ACKNOWLEDGEMENTS

First of all, I'd like to thank my ahh-mazing beta readers: Jenna, Helen, Alisha, Jesika, Keri, Laura, Jessica, and Leanne. This is my first foray into reverse harem books, and you sexy ladies helped me choose just the right details to make this story shine.

Oh, and thank you for licking the dragon. ;)

To my wonderful Editor, Ms. T. Thank you for working tirelessly with me to get everything just so.

Christian Bentulan, you make the world's most beautiful covers. I love this one so much, and I can't wait to see the next!

To the Lovers of Haret ARC Team - thank you for reading and reviewing in time for my release day! And to the beauties who hang out in the Lovers group, you're my BFFs now. I'm never letting you go.

Finally, thank you to my wonderful family, who don't read the books (thank the stars). Y'all bear with me and my wandering eye for a story. Without your support and Starbucks, none of these stories would come to life.

ABOUT THE AUTHOR

Laurel Chase lives in the state that boasts of fast horses,
fast cars, and fast women.
She writes steamy romance and lives in her head more and
more each day – hey, the scenery is great in there.
She never sleeps enough, and she drinks too much coffee,
but she'd never replace any of that with sensible stuff.

Find her hanging out on social media,
usually in the Lovers of Haret readers' group!

Made in the USA
Monee, IL
05 September 2020

41344453R00154